CW01022089

# FORESHORE
## Classic Short Fiction

# About
# H J Taylor Salmon

Henry Salmon lives in Stratford-upon-Avon, England with his wife and two daughters. His love of creating worlds in his imagination has led to this debut novel. He is currently working on a second Aurelia story. Henry is also a music teacher, musician, and piano technician.

H J TAYLOR SALMON

# THE GATES OF AURELIA

FORESHORE PUBLISHING
London

Published by Foreshore Publishing 2022.
The home of quality short fiction.

Copyright © H J Taylor Salmon 2022

This book is sold subject to the condition that it shall not,
by way of trade or otherwise, be lent, re-sold, hired out, or
otherwise circulated without the publisher's prior consent
in any form of binding or cover other than that in which
it is published and without a similar condition, including
this condition, being imposed on the subsequent purchaser
Foreshore Publishing

The Forge 397-411 Westferry Road,
Isle of Dogs, London, E14 3AE

Foreshore Publishing Limited Reg. No. 13358650

ISBN 978-1-9168790-7-2

www.foreshorepublishing.com

Dedicated to Nicky, Elizabeth and Rebecca.
But also to Avril, I didn't realise
how much you influenced and
were a part of me until you were gone.

# Chapter I

THUNDEROUS RUMBLES STRUCK ABOVE Philip's head, caused by what he assumed to be the footsteps of a crowd of drunk Ranians enjoying their new life here. Shouting and singing was muffled by the wooden floorboards and iron frame above. Their songs were of victory still, even after a year of occupation, they sang of their unforeseen triumph over Aurelia; a day Philip would never forget. The thunderous steps above was a reminder of that day as he heard the ships crash down from Lepan's atmosphere, signalling the losing battle above the skies.

It was almost a full sun's orbit to the day that it began. Philip remembered that day well. It had been rumoured days before of Rana's intentions to invade the Aurelian colony. The people of Lepans couldn't foresee how Aurelia's fleet could be defeated; until the unthinkable happened.

There was much anticipation in the air that day, Philip remembered, the excitement of hearing about the mighty Suns of War, Aurelia's pride of the fleet, the conquering heroes. It was reported that ruthless Admiral Carne led Rana's fleet. When the roaring thunder began reverberating in the skies, it was almost like the fulfilling of the Prophecy of Forcewild: *Then in the sky I heard the sound of great thunder roaring like a wild beast ready to attack. I saw other worlds alight with fire: it filled the skies destroying all in its path. In the flames I heard the screams of armies dying, filled with rage and hatred, they tore each other apart.* His father had read that passage during the prayer meeting the night before, as some in the village had been consumed with fear. That day had started off so clear, the blue sky a picturesque moment of tranquility. But it seemed the clouds heard what was going on above them and soon the blue sky became a sea of grey, the premonition of a storm, Philip had heard some say. He had heard his younger sister Nanni, who was three orbits past the sun younger than Philip was, and a lot more naive. She believed it was the clouds getting ready to catch the falling ships to stop them from hitting the ground too hard. Her sweet high voice had so much innocence. Philip shed a tear as he remembered her face and how cute her little puffed cheeks were. Dayala Creda, his father, would always sing with Nanni, Philip didn't admit it at the time, but he enjoyed listening to it. It was the sound of home and a contrast to the dark damp cellar he now had to stay in until he was told. Philip's father was the Minister, a Reverend to the Holy Faith of Jei, Lord of Lords, creator of all things.

Sterling grey eyes like a calm ocean that would look on Philip with such pride, Dayala Creda was not a tall man, nor was he short. Philip thought that he might one day soon be taller than his father, maybe when he was eighteen orbits past the sun; right now, he was only fourteen and still only a boy in everyone's eyes.

There was much his father taught him, mostly all about the love, mercy, and compassion of Jei. His father taught him how to cook over a fire and use homegrown herbs and spices brought at market to get the best flavour from the meat. Amongst the more joyful things Philip remembered was how his father helped him climb trees. Ever since Philip was young, he often went for the closest tree to climb. His father would help him and give instructions as to where to put his feet. As Philip got older it turned into, "who can get up to the highest point the fastest?" That was until Dayala's back went one harvest, when he was unable to lift or carry anything too heavy for weeks. Dayala declared himself retired from tree climbing, instead Philip always saw the smile from his ivory face beaming towards Philip sat at the highest point of any tree he climbed.

With so much humility flowing through his blood, Philip remembered the kindness and hope he gave to many. The night before, while some feared for what was to come, it was Dayala who gave hope. He would read and pray from the Amel Cristea. His favourite passage from the Songs of Anani:

*"You are the melody, the unchanging symphony. The author of song and composer of harmony. Many have tried to change your work, still the song is sung in your creation. When those around me hurt and mock me, you are the shield that protects me. Even when I turn away, you are always waiting for me. You long to hold me and you never stop loving me, the darkest night can't hide your light.*

*As the day turns to night and the night turns to day, your love is never torn from me.*

*Everywhere I go you are always by my side, there is nowhere I can go, from you I cannot hide.*

*You are the melody, the unchanging symphony. Will you please forgive me, for all that I say and do wrong.*

*Every chance you give me, lets me know you care for me. Even though the journey's road is winding and long.*

*You are the melody, where the universe is in harmony. You are the giver of light. The song of worlds who sings for me, let me keep singing in your harmony. The darkest night can't hide your light.*

*There beside me each and every day, your love lights the path of my way. Your face is like the brightest sun lighting up the worlds and everything that's good inside me. You are the beacon for troubled ships in the bay. Drawing us closer each and every day."*

Time was endless. The only light he saw was round the corner of one of the inner walls, a double door of rotten wood that let in such a draft, the only place he could go was to cuddle up to himself and an old moth-eaten rug that smelt of flood water. The only other door was a double hatchway that led into the bar above his head. Every so often Voi Heia, the Gicelian bar man would come down to change the barrels or check if the pumps for the ale were still working. There was little to do in the cellar. Philip wondered if it was true what they said about Gicelians, that they were all pale of skin with long white stringy hair. It was said Gicela was cold, freezing even, some had said it was as cold as Fylaxi the prison planet, others had said it was colder; Philip had not the nerve to ask.

There was little else in the cellar, save his torn blue t-shirt, with the holes exposing his ivory skin to the stale air. He felt unclean. There had been no chance of a wash of any sort since he had been smuggled into Landburness a few days before. His hands were dirty and had run them through his wavy caramel hair. The brown shoes he had worn all the way through his ordeal were coming apart, being almost able to pull the soles off completely.

Vivid images of the Ranian attack on the oval shaped beige carriage he and another villager had taken to escape the village still haunted him. Mandel, the man who had helped Philip, had shown so much kindness, risking everything and paying the price for it. Now his grave would forever be the ruins of the carriage out in the middle of the plains. Philip had managed to hide himself amongst some rocks close to where they had been stopped. Once Ranian troops had left, Philip travelled as much as he could at nighttime, using the darkness to hide his skin colour from the Ranian invaders.

The hatch above Philip opened. Down came Voi Heia: his tall and muscular figure clothed in a tight black shirt and black trousers, the likes of Philip had never seen. His arms were like small tree trunks bearing muscles so thick, Philip wondered if he could even get his two hands around them. Voi gave a look to Philip, placing a single finger to his pale lips, an instruction not to make a sound. Philip's heart started to race. The blood pumped and beat louder and louder with his breath sounding heavier and heavier each moment the hatchway was open. Voi lifted heavy crates of ale, wine and spirits, lifting them up effortlessly like they were no weight at all. Once they were up, the Gicelian reached up his arms and pulled himself up back into the bar. Nerves calmed. It was when the main delivery came that Philip really panicked, he was told, "wrap up in the old carpet. You mustn't be seen or heard by anyone!" It was a warning Philip had heeded. Already he had seen too much a boy his age should never see. So much hatred from one race to another. Punishments from the conquerors were lashed out to those whose crimes are merely living and believing in something else.

It was those times he wished his Mother and Father were here with him, even his older sister Rija, when she wasn't trying to tell Philip what to do all the time, she gave great hugs, especially when they were needed. But there were none of his family around. All had been separated a few weeks ago, giving Philip the task he set out to do: rescue his sisters and leave Lepans, never to come back.

From his once beige trousers, he took a piece of paper. It had been carefully folded and looked after more than any money that he could have come into possession with. Carefully he unfolded it and read the words silently in his head:

*Then I saw from the ashes a new city rise up from the sun's burning rays. The city was made of pure gold where the descendant, who was like a mighty bird, but also a humble one, that changed from its hunting ways to reign. There it sat on the throne and began a glorious reign over the stars and land; its name given was 'peace.' For all those who read these words, this dark time will challenge all those who keep faith in Jei. The time will pass, peace will reign for a time and time again. Jei is the author of all, the one who will right the wrongs of those who seek to destroy.*

It was the last page of the Amel Cristea that his father tore from the book just before Ranian troops came to the village. Dayala knew the fate, which was set for him, even if Philip didn't. Ranian Admiral Carne had placed Marshall Law upon Lepans with the declaration: "Ranian is all you need to be worshipping. There are no gods, only your new masters. The punishment for breaking this, Dayala and Olyssia, Philip's mother, knew, all too well.

Philip read it over and over again. Each time new images came into his mind as to what was being described. Wondering if the Prophet Anani, whose visions are the ones described, saw Lepans and the turmoil that has fallen it. He had also started to believe that this passage was chosen deliberately by his father, not just because it was easy to find in a moment, but he knew it was the light to hold onto in the darkness that would surround his son.

Light faded from the wooden door and darkness fell. He had set the old rug as a pillow and laid his head down. It was hardly the easiest place to sleep, the cold draft became harder with more of a bite to it, he felt it most where his skin was exposed. Even curling himself up in a fetal ball only kept part of the cold off.

There was never any silence in the bar, one rowdy raucous lead to another, with the levels of noise fluctuating throughout the day.

After being awake for much of the night and day, the noise of the bar became a background hum that lured him into a daze before finally relinquishing his mind and thought from consciousness to sleep.

Sounds of all sorts whispered and muttered around him waking him from his partial sleep. It was always at the point of deep sleep that a knock or a bang, even the sound of a distant engine turning off would startle him again. Rattling hammered from wood. Not from the hatch, even though the bar was still busy, it came from the other doors. The creak made Philip a little nervous, while intrigued at the same time. Philip stayed where he was but sat up cowering more into the shadows of the corner of the cellar.

Whoever was coming was having to force the door open as the wood scraped against the cold stone floor. Light footsteps followed before a hooded figure in black presented themselves as if they knew Philip was here. Tall and well-built was the shadow in front of the young man, the hood shrouded their face, but it stared like a ghost towards Philip's direction. A long dark coat was brushed by the overpowering draft that came in through the door. Philip shivered his teeth were chattering. He watched this figure head back towards the door and close it.

After the draft dropped and a little heat started to build up gradually again, the figure came back into the main part of the cellar. The hood was lifted down revealing a man, someone who Philip was waiting for. "George! You're back!" Philip said with such excitement.

Philip met George Lawson Quinn after a trip into Landburness with a few of the other villagers. It was on the same day the battle took place above them. A small piece of ship fell from the sky and landed in the Andefera river a few miles away but caused a shockwave that destroyed the bridge into the city. It meant Philip and the other villagers had to travel for miles to find the next crossing, which happened to be the village where he met George and Tabatha Lawson Quinn.

They were missionaries working in the Avian Republic and were visiting friends of theirs in the village. George had said he and Tabatha had visited Lepans a lot, it was almost a second home away from the trials that they faced regularly on Diasos. Rana's invasion of Lepans brought an all too familiar sight back to them.

Philip had remembered the way back to that village in the hope that George and Tabatha could help him rescue his sisters. Once he had found the couple, George had smuggled him here to wait for what the next move would be.

George headed over to Philip and knelt beside him. "I have managed to get a ship to smuggle you out of here. An old friend of mine, Sago Lathreos. He is going to take you and some others we have rescued. He will take you to Aurelia's gates. It's important that you tell Aurelia what's happening here."

"Who is he? How do you know him?" Philip asked.

"He has helped us many times. By trade, he is a trader: he buys goods from planet to planet then sells them elsewhere. But he has often smuggled the

Amel Cristea in for us many times to places where it's not allowed. He is a good man," George confirmed, hoping to reassure Philip.

Philip gave a dejected look. His eyes widened, moaning like a wanting animal. "What about my sisters? He asked. "Do you know?" It was the news he had been waiting for since he arrived here.

His grown-up friend had a plain stare from his blue eyes, Philip found it hard to read, and so started to believe the worst. "Sago says he knows a man, Tais, from Diasos in the Avian Republic. According to Sago, he poses as a trader, but it's a front for smuggling Telsi and other addictive substances the Galaxy has to offer. This Tais has bragged and tried to drag Sago down to this house. Apparently, there has been an arrival of new girls, at least that's what Tais has said. It's the only lead we have. I'm going to go and check it out. How have you been here? Has Voi given you food?" George asked.

A gentle nod answered George. "Can I come? I can be quiet and careful," Philip pleaded.

Still George was inscrutable. "It's dangerous. We only walk the streets at night. It's the only way Law Enforcement and the troops don't recognise us. If you are caught, you get shot!" George sighed at the sight of Philip's face dropping gravely with the cellar now seemingly looking and feeling lonelier and colder than it was before.

"Please!" Philip pleaded again. "How are you going to identify my sisters? It would be quicker if I came with you." It was a last-ditch attempt to convince his friend and ally into allowing him to go. Scrunching his face as if he knew it was a bad idea and allowing the young man to come along went against his better judgment, George reluctantly nodded his head. Philip threw his arms around him, muttering words of thanks over and over again. "You will need to wear something warmer and something darker to walk through the shadows of the city. Troops and Law Enforcement are out in their droves. You are not the only one trying to get off Lepans," George warned.

Philip's eyes had adjusted better to the darkness, and with it, the view of the porcelain skinned tall missionary stood up, bending slightly unable to straighten up due to the low ceiling. Gently he knocked on the hatchway, then sat back down next to Philip.

They both waited. In the time they waited George took a picture out of his pocket it was of a boy about the same age as Philip. In the darkness it was hard to see, but the reflection of the gloss paper reflected small amounts of light that shone through the holes in the hatchway.

"Is that your son?" Philip enquired. "I remember your wife talked about him a lot. He is the same age as me, isn't he?"

George looked fondly at the picture with a heartbroken complexion unable to hide in the dark. "Yes," he replied. "We spoke to him just before the invasion, almost a full suns' orbit ago now. We haven't been able to see or speak to him since."

"Where is he?"

"In the fleet. His Grandfather is training him up to be a fleet officer. I'm sure one day he will have his own ship to command; whether I will see that day, only Jei knows."

Their conversation was disturbed by Voi climbing down to them. He moved his pale face, so pale that even in the dark you could see it. "What's wrong?" He whispered to George.

"We need more clothes for Philip, we are going to try and find his sisters. But I can't take him out in those things," George gestured to Philip's attire. "Have you got anything suitable and preferably with a hood?"

"I'll see what I can do," Voi said. He lifted a crate of wine up through the hatch then pulled himself back up with his huge muscles straining and almost twice, if not three times the size of Philip's arm.

Again Philip and George waited. They knew Voi couldn't just go and get clothes. The bar was packed, and he didn't want to draw any attention to the Aurelians underneath the floor in the cellar.

"Where's Tabatha?" Philip asked to fill the silence, curious to know of George's wife.

"She is trying to smuggle food to families who are starving since Rana's take over. Rana has banned all Aurelians from buying food or anything. She has also found some other children that need smuggling out. We will hopefully meet with them at the port in a day or so."

"When we were on Diasos, there was a law created by the Avian Republic that gave you a stamp which allowed you to buy food and supplies. This stamp marked you as a worshiper of the Chancellor. There were many of the faith of Jei who refused to bow to the Avian Republic. We have seen Jei being faithful to those who honour him so much. So many are reliant on the love and support that provides what needs they can. We met many traders who were heroes of the faith of Jei, they would spend what little profits they got, on helping these people. We got to meet a number of these people. We prayed with them and looked after them as much as we could," George added.

"I believe Jei will be faithful here too. We just must continue to pray, pray every day for the bread and water we need to survive. But there are many children who are suffering terribly. Like yourself, their parents have been killed, or have died, because of Rana's ruling. It's not right they, or anyone for that fact, should live with this. Tabatha has made it her mission to take any child and help them escape and try and get them to Aurelia, where they will be looked after properly."

"How were you allowed into Diasos if they were against anyone of the faith of Jei?" Asked Philip. All his life he had only known contentment and peace. Life in the city was very different to that in the villages, it was more complex, Philip thought, with more complex challenges which Philip felt he needn't trouble himself with. Since the invasion, Philip found himself growing up faster trying to understand the evolving world around him and the complexities it brought. "I had a job as an engineer for a company out there, that was to be our cover. I was headhunted for the role, Tabatha and I saw an opportunity to spread the word and love of Jei to those around us. We knew it would be near impossible, but we felt it was what we were called to do."

The hatchway opened again, only slightly this time, and down came some clothes: a black long coat with a dark hooded top. Philip put them straight on. When he was ready, George Lawson Quinn led him through the cellar. With much care, George opened the rotten doors: they were long with six small windows grouped together at the top.

It was those six windows that had provided all the light for the cellar, Philip thought, and that it was a dire rotten door, that would have only taken a firm blow from something solid to bash it open, that had hidden him from the terror that awaited them in the open streets of Landburness.

Night was in full flow. Stars were barely visible, polluted by the artificial light of the streets and buildings. George and Philip crept up the uneven stone stairs watching nervously for any other being that might be out at night.

The back of the bar was a wasteland full of rubbish: old bottles, glasses, wrappers and discarded food. Vermin were roaming amongst the remains scavenging like the starving former Aurelian colonists of Lepans, now considered vermin themselves by their new overlords.

Philip felt the cold of night even more with his blood freezing inside, not helped by distant occasional gun fire. It was the sign of another Aurelian trying to survive the despair of Lepans, only to see their life abruptly ended at the hand of the ruthless troops of Rana.

# Chapter II

A GLORIOUS LIGHT BECKONED over the Great Plains of Lepans: it covered the green fields and golden crops that went on for miles making the hills set in the distance like lighthouses set on the border from one laed to the next.

The wooden log houses of the village were light brown, coated in a mustard smelling solution to preserve the wood through the winter storms that were coming. Flowers of bright colours with strong rich stems filled gardens of the many houses of the village.

Community was at the heart of the village. They grew crops together and shared the livestock and harvests each year. Any problems were faced as one and any celebration was revelled in, as one.

Wreaths of pure white and pink flowers were out in full display upon staffs set in the grass surrounding a congregation of handmade wooden empty chairs. It was at the heart of the village, the centre of the community. Around the village there was much rushing around, much had to be prepared: a large feast was being made for all to join, but before that, a legerteam union between two of the village's residents.

Philip sat on the old log that was a bench for all to sit around the fire. He watched the village men dress in their finest suits, while the ladies and girls wore their stolas. Mandel sat down next to Philip, his black curly hair was a mess, and his rugged chubby round face had a week's long growth of hair around his mouth and chin. His long suit jacket was blue, matching the skies above. On it were embroidered yellow globe-like flowers sewn into the sleeve and lapels; his waistcoat matched the jacket, while his dark yellow trousers were verging on the shade of brown, covered over by black boots.

Mandel was merry, clasping a tankard of ale brewed within the village. "There are days when I wish I was back in the fleet. There was none of this," Mandel said, waving his tankard around at the madness consuming the village. "All I had to do was to get up and go to the engines and keep the ship running."

"Were you really in the Aurelian Fleet?" Philip asked, his eyes in awe of the elder man.

"That I was. I started off in the Star of War Vega. Then I was transferred to the Sun of War Vesuvius. It was a grand ship, the size of a city. Have you ever seen one?" Mandel asked, taking a sip of his ale.

"No. But I have often wondered what it would be like. What does it look like?" Philip asked. He longed to have an image of Aurelia's master warship to fuel his imagination. While he would wander off outside the village to the nearby woods, his thoughts would become daydreams of him on the ships flying through space.

Mandel got out a small picture that he carried around with him. It showed a large ship with a barrel- like body, housing over a thousand cannons on its side. At the front was a head shape, like a wild beast with a large snout. "That's what it looks like. I took this picture the day I walked onto it at Burloca station on Aurelia. I will never forget that day; my proudest moment."

"What do you miss about the fleet?" Enquired Philip.

"I was always amazed by space: from leaving the systems travelling into the red, almost sunburst mists of the Gang of Saltus, that's what separates the seven systems of Jubal. To get from here in the

Dorian system to Aurelia in the Ionian system, you must travel through the Gang. What a sight it is. If you ever go into it you will see what I mean," replied Mandel, remembering fondly his previous life. His brown eyes stared as if staring into space itself seeing the images he described.

Before Philip could ask any more questions, a voice called his name from across the grass.

Philip looked and saw his mother, Olyssia. "Philip! You need to get ready! The legerteam is starting soon. Where are your sisters?" She asked.

"I think they are helping father out," responded Philip.

"Well go and fetch them. They both must put their maids' dresses on." Philip ran off heading towards the village hall: the hall was longer than any of the houses in the village but only had one floor, with a gable roof of carefully fixed logs and cooked dirt to seal the gaps. Inside was an open space where a table had been laid out with many different meats and crops freshly prepared for the festivities to follow.

"Father!" Philip called out as he saw him sneak some of the small meat rolls into his mouth. He looked around at his son with a guilty look in his grey eyes.

"I was just making sure they were cooked properly," he said. That was what he always said anytime he got caught. Philip's mother would always warn her husband he would start growing a bigger waistline, still his father didn't take any notice, that's why his blue trousers had to be adjusted for the third time in the last few days.

"Mother wants Rija and Nanni. They must go and get ready."

"RIJA…NANNI…!" His father shouted out.

Rija walked out from a kitchen with Nanni quickly in tow, both wearing dresses: Rija wore a white short sleeved dress that went down to her ankles, decorated with a consistent pattern of grey horizontal stripes. Nanni wore her favourite dress of clustering red, pink and blue flowers on purple cloth.

Nanni was beaming a smile, showing her painted nails to her brother. "Look what Rija did for me. She even put a little bit of colour onto my eyes. She says we are going to look like princesses." Nanni paused for a moment and looked up to her big sister. "Do you remember when the High King visited?" The young girl said switching from one subject to another. "I remember when he visited Landburness going through the streets in his carriage. I remember dressing up for him and standing in the crowd watching him go by."

"That was three or five sun's orbits, ago," Rija remarked wondering where her little sister was going with her train of thought.

"Will he come again? I quite like dressing in pretty dresses," Nanni said cheerfully.

Dayala gave his daughter a cuddle squeezing the love into her. "I'm afraid, Healicnes High King Arius V will not come to Lepans for another ten sun's orbits or so. But you will have plenty of legerteams to go to. You never know your sister might have one soon," he said looking over at his eldest. Rija shied away a little, her amber hair dropped over her eyes. She brushed her hair back behind her right ear. "Come on Nanni, we need to go get ready," Rija said, smiling at her sister.

Philip followed behind them. It was only a few minutes walk to the house, but in the time it took them to walk, Nanni had not stopped talking: "Will you teach me how to plait my hair, can you teach me how to draw and paint? Then can you draw a picture of me in my stola for the wedding?" She asked whilst holding her sister's hand.

Nanni was so excited as she walked along, there was a definite excitable bounce to her step. Rija just smiled and laughed at how excited Nanni was getting. When they got back to the house all three went to get ready.

Philip was ready within a few minutes: he wore a dark green long jacket that went down to his knees, with a maroon waistcoat, white shirt, and brown cravat. His mother had handed him a new pair of cream-coloured trousers to go under his dark brown boots. He felt a little uncomfortable; his mother looked at him so proudly, tilting her head to the side and thought how grown up he looked. "You are going to be a very handsome man," she said, kissing his forehead, "almost a spitting image of your father when I first met him."

"Does everyone on Aurelia really wear this?" Philip asked, snarling a little. "I don't know what's wrong with what I was wearing before?"

"Because those dirty blue trousers you keep wearing are very worn and they are better for the harvest picking than occasions such as today. Yes, they do wear this on Aurelia, Babil and all over Jubal. Now stop your moaning."

In the background Philip had noticed the holographic computer displaying images of news throughout Jubal. He tried to listen out to what was being said but his mother had turned the sound down so much that only murmurs could be heard. His eyes were drawn to the image of a large Aurelian warship in a station. It was in the background of a reporter.

"That's a Sun of War!" Philip said enthusiastically. "Mandel showed me what one looks like. He used to work on one." His voice sunk a little low when he realised what the report was probably about. "Is it the war?" He said turning to his mother.

Olyssia quickly turned the computer off. Her complexion dropped a little. "Yes," she said softly, "Aurelia attacked Rana ships at Romus in the Lydian system. Rana's Consul, Proxenos has said there will be retaliation for Aurelia's aggression."

"But didn't Rana attack Hilderas in the Phrygian system? And didn't they attack a civilian cruiser?" Philip asked his mother.

"This war between Aurelia and Rana has been going on and on with each side retaliating to each other's attack," Olyssia said gravely. "It was all because of an assassination of Rana's Consul Ocissus some suns' orbits ago now. Rana blamed Aurelia for it, but no one could prove it and it remains a mystery to this day."

Olyssia sighed. "Look, don't think about it. Today is a day of celebration. Is your father dressed and ready? He is taking the service."

"Not yet," Philip replied, "he was making sure the meat had been cooked properly." His mother raised her brow unsurprised by her husband's actions.

She sent him off to fetch him and to tell him to get ready. The ceremony came and the village all sat in the handmade chairs. The white and pink flowers had decorated the sides of the chair and down the aisle. Many bright colours from the gentlemen's suits and the women's bright coloured stolas added to the joy on display for the day.

All fell quiet as the music played from string instruments at the front. Down the aisle walked Nanni, her face made up beautifully making her look older than she was. She was followed by Rija, both in a strapless peach stola with a matching ribbon acting as a belt high up the waist.

Two other girls who were slightly older than Rija walked down next followed by a girl dressed in white. They all stopped at the front where Philip's father stood with the leather bound Amel Cristea open in his hand.

The legerteam had started with words to tie two people together:

*Condel Secan, we are gathered for the union of souls. For here in the presence of Jei and the power of his love, we commit you both. All are loved from the very start, who Jei unites together, no one can part. In kindness, in patience, in unselfishness, love is always present and the greatest power there is.*

Rija stood up to the side of the congregation with the other maids. In a three-part harmony they sang:

*Let this kiss be sweeter than wine, more perfect than a rose.*
*Sealed this day till your Lord calls you home.*
*Where once was two, now leave here as one;*
*You join together to make your own flesh and bone.*

*Everyday you'll be together, from dawn all through the day.*
*With each dusk a new day dawns, what new feats you will see.*
*Be the love, be the light for both of you to dwell.*
*Surrender who you are to love, and set yourselves free.*

Philip had never realised how beautiful Rija's voice was until then, especially as she sang with the others. The sound had captivated all those with ears to hear. He overheard someone else saying it was like listening to the choristers at the Temple of Jei in Vortigern on Aurelia, the way each melody line could have stood alone by itself, but here it joined with others to create the most beautiful sound.

The ceremony was over, and the festivities had begun. There was much merriment and joy, dancing and singing. The drums played loud as did the

Pluccian, the great string instrument that plucked and strummed along to the rhythm of the drums.

Philip watched as Nanni and Rija danced together still in their peach stolas. Nanni had not let her sister sit down and always demanded one more dance. Every now and again he would catch Rija casting an eye over a boy or young man the same age as her. He was suited still with his cravat nowhere to be seen, his shirt undone at the top, still wearing his brown waistcoat and jacket making him look smart and handsome. He had often heard her talk about him and how he wanted to head into Landburness to study business. Rija herself had talked of heading there to study art, trying to convince her parents that it was for the course, not because he was going there. Philip had been in the room when it had been discussed, his mother asked her if she would consider studying in Vortigern at Aurelia's most prestigious arts college. For now she was undecided and had still another sun's orbit to decide.

Mandel dropped himself down next to Philip again. He was sluggish in his movement and slurring some of his words. His suit was a mess: waistcoat open, cravat and jacket nowhere to be seen. "How many have you had?" Philip asked.

"Quite probably too many," he said drunk, bringing up bubbles of air. "While there is ale to drink, I will always be there to drink it!" He took a large sip, gulping much of what was left in his tankard down.

Night was already in full swing. The bonfire was burning at the heart of the village. Flames and lights lit up the paths to the houses like stars shining from the ground. Philip turned to Mandel knowing his history. There was a hesitation within him to ask but it kept pressing on him. "Can Aurelia win this war?" Mandel took another large gulp. "There is no ship that can come up against one Sun of War. Then just imagine what would happen if they faced a fleet of them: Eversor, Olympus, Mars, Katato, of course Vesuvius, you name them. They are the greatest ships in Jubal. That's why Rana keeps fighting. They want the authority over space and the Gang of Saltus that Aurelia has. But they will never get it, at least not while the Suns of War, the pride of the Aurelian fleet is about."

Neither spoke for a few moments. "Is it a hard life in the Aurelian fleet?" Philip asked.

"Hard? Yes! Imagine being pushed to your limits and then having to go on. But when the battle is raging around you; it makes you feel alive. It's no easy time, but I have missed it sometimes." Mandel got up, putting his tankard down by his side, empty of ale. Philip watched him go and fill it up from a barrel outside the village hall.

An arm reached out while Philip wasn't looking and dragged him into the dance. "Come on brother!" Philip looked round and saw Rija's smiling face pulling him along. "Nanni wants to dance with us both. You know how she enjoys dancing; I've been dancing with her all evening."

Philip and his siblings danced. To the side of the dance, his mother and father stood, watching their children with such enjoyment and love. He then saw a man pull his father away, Philip thought nothing of it until a voice started shouting: "THEY ARE COMING!! RANA IS COMING!"

The music stopped and all eyes glared at this man. The darkness hit his face, but in his voice, there was much fear. He brought his figure by the fire surrounding himself with the villagers.. His silhouette before the fire was like a shadow in the night, haunting the village with a prophecy many had read and dreaded the day it would come to pass.

His voice softened with all eyes cast upon him: "The Governor of Lepans has just issued a warning: a Ranian fleet under Admiral Carne has left Juru and has crossed the Denisses Belt.

They will be orbiting Lepans by nightfall tomorrow."

# Chapter III

WHISPERS OF A KNOWN fear patrolled the streets. Hovering transport vehicles droned distantly and close through the night. George and Philip tentatively headed down the dark alley between the bar and a block of houses. It was known that all Aurelians had been banished from the city, that Lepans was to be a Ranian colony. Steadily, over the first sun's orbit since the invasion, Rana had begun their colonisation. Weary of spying eyes from the windows above, George knew the importance of the shadows.

The first twenty yards through the shadows of two buildings calmed Philip's nerves a little, but deep down inside he knew the biggest challenge was yet to come. When they reached the street, lamps lit patches of circled light along the road. It reflected onto the buildings showing off the wall scrawl written by conquering Ranians lavishing their victory over their sworn enemy, mixed with Aurelian messages of defiance against the conquerors. The way through was unclear. Each moment, transport vehicles sounded closer or got further away; neither George nor Philip knew which.

Philip watched George Lawson Quinn closely: his eyes scanned the terrain slowly with a thought to every sound that could be heard near and far. He put up his black hood, Philip copied and followed George as he went left, running light footed from one shadow to the other, each time throwing his back up against the stone of an over-scrawled building.

It was the same process through a great number of streets, the view Philip saw was more or less the same: buildings that Philip knew to be grey stone had been almost trashed from their original look. A war of words and threats between two races was displayed openly on many walls. Property had been vandalised by one or the other, no doubt in retaliation for a previous offence against the other. It was a far distant memory now that Philip had of these streets, he barely recognised them. It was like he was in a foreign land that he had never stepped foot in before and had no idea where he was going, or if there was a way out. Still their journey went on.

Three or four times they found themselves ducking for cover into some dark alley or behind some structure, camouflaging themselves from the light while hovering transport vehicles went by on patrol: their viridian green scaled skin were heavily armoured and armed with guns ready for a battlefield.

The occasional gunshots heard in different streets suggested that maybe this was more of a battlefield than Philip first thought. A few times in the distance he had seen shapes of what looked like bodies left to rot in the street. He wondered if that was to be their grave or would someone take pitty on their remains and give them a burial; it was more likely, he thought, that the Ranian troops would just dump the bodies in a wasteland somewhere with all the other waste. It was a horrid thought and one Philip quickly dismissed.

The sight of the bodies didn't do anything for his nerves. He found himself praying to Jei, whispering in his head the same phrase: "Condel Secan, Drythen, please protect me. Please let me just get to my sisters. Please let them be safe." The more he muttered it in his head, the more the muttering became a desperate plea, almost crying to himself contemplating the worst that he might find.

How long they had been sneaking through the city was anyone's guess. It was still night, and the troops were still out on patrol. A few more times they had to take cover, hide, and wait for transport vehicles to pass. Philip wondered how many times George had done this, he seemed to have an instinct for it, that gave Philip much confidence.

Tall buildings of the city centre were instantly recognised by Philip, although he thought they looked defiled and like an empty shell, as if all life in them had been taken away. He saw the marketplace where he had helped sell the village produce: the stalls had been vandalised, almost completely destroyed with the fabric of the cloth roofs ripped to shreds.

The city centre was a few blocks away now, with their course set for the other side of the city to where the cellar was. Philip had stayed behind George all the way. For a moment, Philip lost himself in his thoughts, he found it a coping mechanism to fend off fear, so far it had worked. "Hide! Quick!" George shouted in a hurried whisper.

He ran, throwing himself into a front garden. Philip followed quickly but the drone of a transport vehicle came in from behind them. Philip heard it: his heart beat faster, his lungs gave him more power than he could have imagined and ran towards the waist high wall George had jumped over.

Philip attempted the jump, but he didn't swing his leg up enough and he just fell back to the floor. He panicked, attempting again to get over the wall. He tried for a third time but failed. Tremors in all his muscles started shaking him, fear rising within that he might not get over the wall in time. The gateway was only a few yards away, but the gate could make a noise disturbing anyone in the building and inadvertently alerting Ranian troops to their position.

George realised Philip was in trouble: he stood up, grabbed Philip's arms, and dragged his whole body over the wall, placing his head on the broken stone surface while his legs temporarily flung in the air. As quick as he could, George pulled the legs down, just as he saw Ranian troops in a coupe shaped hovering transport vehicle come down the street. The vehicle paused on the road close to where they were.

Heavy boots stomped onto the ground. Light metal clashed like tiny metal chains with each step taken. The words both Aurelians dreaded: "I thought I saw something!" Spoken by the Ranian soldier as his steps got nearer and nearer. Silently, whilst lying down, George pushed his back up against the wall. Trying to flatten himself out as much as possible, he prompted Philip to do the same. The light of the streetlamp couldn't touch them, the wall was too high. Philip closed his eyes and prayed silently again: "Please hide us! Please hide us! Let no light nor eye see us! Please, Condel Secan! Please, Drythen!"

The boots stopped! By George's reckoning, the soldier was within a yard of the wall they had leapt over. There was no sound for an agonising few seconds. Then a step came closer and the sound of eyes peering over the wall.

"It was an animal! Someone's pet!" A growling impatient voice from the vehicle shouted.

There was a delay…then the footsteps walked away back to the transport vehicle.

Neither George nor Philip gave any sigh of relief until they had heard the drone disappear far off in the distance. Slowly, with great care and attention they lifted themselves over and back onto the street. "Keep your eyes and ears open!" George warned. They started to move on again.

Streetlamps had started to become more scarce, few and far between. The city centre was long behind them, and the outskirts of the city was nearer at hand. It was a rough part of the city, even before the invasion it had been: "a place of thieves and devilry!", those who had travelled to market with him would say.

Here it was easier to sneak about. Few transport vehicles seemed to come by. Perhaps there was nothing here for them to have any reason to come? Philip thought. He asked himself a question, answering it himself, remembering then what happened the last time he wasn't paying attention.

Walking freely down the street through the dark, the only light to be seen was from the houses along both sides, they were all bunched up together cramming as many buildings as they could in. Philip had been told that this part of town was always supposed to be temporary. When an influx of people came here, there was nowhere for them to stay.

These houses were quickly erected awaiting a permanent residency; these permanent residences never happened.

Houses were very square like they were cubes of concrete that someone had just carved out the inside to make special rooms. There was no garden space that Philip could see and guessed that round the back would be a similar story.

George led the way to another street that was the same. This whole part of the city looked like there were endless blocks of streets all the same, everywhere the eyes turned, the same view was seen.

Noise like talking could be heard and music like a thumping beat muffled by walls started to grow louder. Philip had started to hear it when they had entered this street, if not faintly from the street before; but the talking was new to his ear. Philip noticed George's pace became more careful again as his steps took him to the side of the street where the noise was coming from.

Lights could be seen and many figures that were Ranians, some in civilian clothing, others were soldiers. They were sitting on chairs, tables and benches smoking herbs in a cig. Cautiously, George slowed up, deliberately keeping his distance, and made sure his hood covered his face and skin. Philip stopped by him. "Why have we stopped?" Philip whispered as he and George suddenly looked at a building on the opposite side of the street from them trying not to be noticed.

"That's the house Tais has bragged about. Apparently, there are twenty or so rooms each one has a girl Ranians imprisoned in there." George replied, staring intently at the building. It was built differently to the other buildings. It was like it had been a farmhouse sometime ago before this part of the city had been developed. The main building has a gable roof and two storeys high; this was the main part of the bar and where the loud music was coming from. Behind that was another building, but it was in an L shape and ran alongside it. Lights were on in all the rooms. They suddenly heard screams and groans coming from the rooms.

"What's happening in there?" Philip asked.

"Best you don't know," George responded quickly.

"Are my sisters in there?" Asked Philip, hopeful that his muttering prayers would be answered.

"I don't know. All I know is that a number of girls have been brought here not too long ago. Your sisters might be amongst them."

Both Aurelians were suddenly caught unawares by a hiss coming from beside them. It was a short sharp hiss, then a low whispered voice addressed them: "WHAT ARE YOU DOING! ARE YOU TRYING TO GET CAUGHT?!" The whispered voice had such bewilderment to it, it was almost angry.

"We're trying to find my sisters," Philip answered back softly.

Both now saw a woman with dark skin and long black braided hair peering out of a window that lacked glass in. A second look saw shards of glass around the vicinity of the window, which made Philip ask what had happened here.

She looked at Philip. He saw her dark brown eyes turn sorrowful towards him. "Come in! Both of you, come in quick," she insisted. George and Philip did as she suggested and snuck in the door without making too much noise so as not disturb the Ranians in the bar opposite.

"What's your name?" George asked politely. He looked around the room they had been invited into. It was as if a bomb had been thrown through the window and gone off. There was shrapnel everywhere with furniture damaged or destroyed.

"Cody, Cody Fliema. I have lived in these terrible streets for many Suns' orbits, but never have I known such horror as to what befalls in that house. What monsters can do that to children?" She asked, her voice became brittle as if her own pain was groaning and surfacing from deep within. "And I ask you… when will Aurelia hear our cries? When will they know of our suffering? When will they know what we have lost here? I have prayed so long now for a reckoning to fall here. For these monsters to fall and die from the swamps from where they came from!" Tears started to form in her eyes and slowly ran down her dark-skinned cheek. Her long blue dress now rags and the remains of what once was a fashionable short sleeve stola.

"Where was Jei when this happened? Where was the one who created all of this? Why does he not intervene, when those who love him are being hurt and treated so wrongfully? Where is he? Why does he not answer my prayers?" She pleaded.

"I don't know," George replied. "But I don't think he ever deserts us, instead he suffers with us. I have been to some of the worst places in the Galaxy and seen unspeakable things. But what I have seen the most, it is in our darkest times, when we see the Love of Jei at work. And it's in the love and actions of strangers and in those who care about us the most."

"Maybe Jei should come down to a normal life!" Cody said angrily. "Let him live in a place where he is discriminated against and hunted because others just don't like him. Let his closest friends betray him and sell him out just so they can save themselves. Then let him be tortured in the most brutal way, then let him be tried in a biased trial and call it justice. Then when he has been executed in the cruellest way, only then can he know of what it is like to live here."

"May I ask...what happened?" George asked softly.

Cody started staring into space, memories flooded back into her mind. "When the ships started landing, all of us around here wondered where all these new people were going to go. Then Carne started dictating the laws. Our worst fears were set after he declared all property was to be confiscated by the new Ranian Government. We thought it would take months to re-house us, but the next day, they came, shooting our windows, kicking in our doors forcing us to grab whatever we could and leave."

"A fight started between us and the troops. We asked where we were supposed to go. They said, 'build your own homes elsewhere. You're not welcome here!' In the fight, my partner got killed, shot three times by Ranian troops. They turned on our houses, threw bombs destroying all that we had. My eldest had ran back into the house, I heard my youngest shout his name and run after him. The bomb exploded, both killed." She wiped tears from her face. The image of her children running into the house still haunting her.

"No Ranian wanted this house. All the others on the street left, heading anywhere where they could go to be free. I stayed here. Searching bins scavenging what scraps of food that I can. Each day I watch that place," she said now staring at the bar across the street, "and I see girl after girl. Some are there for a short while, then sold off, I assume to another owner. While the rest, this is their home now."

Philip was greatly saddened by the woman's tale. He thought of how much he missed his sisters, and wanted desperately to put his family back together while there was still a chance. "My parents were executed," Philip said. Cody turned to face him, taken aback by the young boy's openness. "My father was a Minister, the local one for our village. Since the invasion, he continued to encourage the village to pray for peace, to pray for strength. He knew this time was coming, and knew it was going to be hard. But his faith never once faltered. Even as the gun was pointed to his head, with the whole village watching, and my sisters forced to see what happens when you defy Carne and his laws. Both my mother and father were shot dead, their bodies left to burn."

"How did you escape?" Cody asked. "I have heard they kill any male for the risk of an army rising up."

"I was told to hide in a tree. I saw the whole thing," Philip said. "I saw troops take my sisters and now I want to save them and get off the planet if we can. I want to send a message to Aurelia, to tell them what is happening here. That they need to return and put right what has gone wrong." Philip's eyes had a sparkle of hope in them. In his head, he guessed it might be foolish but while he had heard that they were still alive he kept hope.

"How old are your sisters?" Cody asked, hoping to be helpful to him.

"Rija is my older sister. She is two sun's orbits older, seventeen in total. A slim figure with shiny, almost golden straight hair. Then there is Nanni.

My younger sister. She is eleven sun's orbits with matching hair to her sisters."

"I was told that a load of new girls were recently brought here, two, maybe three days ago. Did you see anything?" George asked Cody.

"Yes. A handful of girls arrived, some even matching your description, but that's all I can tell you. From here you only see the men going in. You don't see any of the girls. Say for the odd small girl who is too little, then they just do chores around the house and wait on the men until they are old enough," Cody said.

Her words filled Philip with even more hope than before. The beings outside the bar had changed, Philip instantly set up a watch, sitting down on glass and shrapnel with his eyes fixed on the bar.

Cody took George to the other room; he gave her some of the food that he had with him as a gesture of how thankful they were to her for her help. He even tried to convince her to leave Lepans, smuggled out and head to Aurelia. Cody was dubious but considered it but would not make the decision at that moment.

Hours ticked by. Soon the night sky began to glimpse a burning skyline that gradually got bigger and gave a natural light to the streets as a new day had begun. Phillip had fallen into a sleep without realising it. But George hadn't and took over the watch.

Men left and others turned up. The music never seemed to stop but changed from one piece to the next seamlessly without anyone knowing. Steadily punters drifted in and out through the day. The three Aurelians in the house opposite subtly watched on, hidden in the room taking it in turns to see if any of the girls could be spotted.

George had managed to spend some time with Cody finding out about her family, in turn he told her about his. Both shared fond memories and hopes they had. Hopes for Lepans and most of all hopes for their own lives.

Time dragged on with little to grab the Aurelians attention. The beats of the bar across the street were almost like the ticking clock, ticking and ticking on and on with no variation to its time or pitch.

Hunger was building amongst the three of them. The supplies George had in his coat pockets had all been exhausted. What he hadn't mentioned to the others was the time limit he had to get Philip and sisters to the port and onto Sago Lathreos's ship. He was a trader, soon his trading front would be done and would need to move on. Time was now counting down. George knew it would be weeks at best before Sago returned.

Philip took his place again spying on the bar. The shape of the two buildings was all too familiar now. He started to notice the delicate details, like the slight arch shape of the wind frames, rotten to the core. All the windows had nets on the other side to stop people looking in or out, whilst still letting in the daylight.

Then there was the space to the right-hand side of the main bar. It was like a mini courtyard, bridging the gap between the bar and part of the L shaped building where all the rooms were. The courtyard was clearly a dumping ground: old barrels and broken bottles were piled up against the walls and across the ground. Broken stones, sheared off from the weight of the heavy barrels constantly placed on them.

Large containers, where the waste had been put, but since the invasion, no refuse collection had happened. Now the bins were overflowing, with rubbish falling out the sides. It wasn't the bins that Philip noticed. A small being with golden amber hair, it was rough and tangled. Below was a long dress of purple cloth that went down as far as her knees decorated with red, pink and blue flowers.

Philip sat bolt upright with his gaze now fixed on the girl hoping she would turn around so he could see her face. It couldn't be the same dress. Nanni always raved that that was her favourite dress and was adamant about wearing it every opportunity she could. It was their mother who had to tell her it needed washing once in a while and that she should save it for special occasions.

It was the day when he last saw his younger sister. The village were to gather to celebrate the harvest, and it was an excuse for all to dress up in their best clothes. Nanni leaped at the chance, even though their mother had put out a light pink stola to wear, Nanni opted for the skirt. Even before daylight was in full force, she had put the dress on. The rest of the family would go downstairs and find her singing away to herself, twirling and dancing to her own song.

When the soldiers took her and Rija away, Philip remembered the thought of his little sister, so overjoyed at being able to wear her favourite dress, would now see it as the most horrific memory. It made him want to find and rescue her even more.

Finally, the small girl turned: it was only slightly to the side, but it was enough to make out her face. It brought an overwhelming sensation of joy; "Nanni is alive!!" He thought to himself and rushed to tell George.

# Chapter IV

STORMS HAD RAGED THROUGH villages and towns, even through the cities. Trees ripped from their roots and shelters blown away. Destructive winds and torrential rain had hammered down. Rivers rose above their banks forming large lakes. Fields and plains had become quagmires almost impassable with thick mud. The winter was passing but still not over, with powerful storms still to come.

Two thirds of a sun's orbit had passed since it was first announced of Rana's intentions. After that everyone's worst nightmares had come to pass. Every life had been affected, and few for the better.

Morning arrived. Philip heard the wind push the rain onto his window. The droplets on the glass were streaming down amidst the thick dark grey clouds consuming the sky. Like a constant irregular beat, the rain tapped, and the wind howled forcing him to wake up. There was noise coming from downstairs, his parents were already up and trying to continue with life as they knew it.

Silently, Philip opened his door and sneaked downstairs. As he walked down the narrow corridor, his parents' voices were channeled a lot more and were clearly audible: "Carne's tyranny has begun!" He heard his father say. "More ships are arriving every day. They have started to move Aurelians out of the cities. I imagine it won't be long until they come for us. Others have said Law Enforcement have started to put an end to prayer meetings and services. I have sent word out to the village that each day we will have a prayer meeting at the start of the day and at the end, but it is to take place in the woods. Everyone needs to choose which one to go to so as not to arouse any suspicion."

Philip walked into the kitchen of their log house. His mother quickly turned the images off from the holographic computer. His father sat at the wooden kitchen table with a deep concentrated thought going through his mind.

"What's going on?" Philip asked.

"Nothing for you to be worried about for now", his mother reassured him. Philip didn't believe her. But since Rana had invaded, his parents had told them information when they needed to know, and Philip trusted that.

Dayala sighed. "Philip, can you go and get Rija and Nanni please." Philip went. He noticed in the corner of his eye as he went back towards the stairs that his mother had turned the news back on. Still, he crept up the stairs and headed for Rija's room first. She was still in her purple nighty with her amber hair wild from a sleepless night. "Mother and father want to see us," he said to her. "Do you know what it's about?" Rija asked.

"No…but it doesn't look good."

Rija slumped down on her bed, her face turned red, and tears started to form in her eyes. "I'm scared. I'm really scared," she said, "it's one thing after another at the moment. They have started to stop all Aurelians going to school or college. All the places are being taken up with Ranians. It's like they are pushing us out and away from everything."

Philip sat down beside her and gently put his arm around her. He didn't really know what to say or if there was anything right to say. "Mother and Father will know what to do. And the village, they are looking out for everyone. I'm sure Aurelia will send a force to take back Lepans soon." Philip had no confirmation of that. He had the idea that Aurelia wouldn't let Rana get away with this and that the fleet would soon arrive to start the fight to regain control. "You don't know that!" Rija snapped. "Why haven't they come already? You've heard the news... their forces are off elsewhere fighting. They have left us here." Philip hung his head.

Refusing to admit it, there was a chance Rija was right; but that was a thought he could not bear to think about and remained hopeful.

"Come on. Let's see what Mother and Father have to say," he said giving Rija a helping hand.

Rija got Nanni, who was clutching her stuffed toy Hengest that had four long white legs and a white long neck. Its soft fur was ruffled, while its ears were made of a silky cloth that Nanni loved the feel of. All three headed down into the kitchen and sat around the rectangular wooden table. Olyssia had something sweet cooking for breakfast, which made Nanni quite excited, so much so she almost threw the Hengest onto the table slamming it down quite hard.

"Your Mother and I need to tell you of what's going on," Dayala said with such a serious face. It had been his complexion for so long now, none of the children could remember when he smiled. "We have heard Ranian troops are moving Aurelians out of the city ready for them to come in. We must know that sooner or later, this might happen here, we just don't know when because we are out in the villages, they may just leave us alone, but there is the possibility that they will move us on too."

"Where will we go?" Nanni asked innocently.

"I don't know. No one in the village knows. But we will try and all stay together," Olyssia replied.

"There's more..." Dayala said, "it would seem that Admiral Carne doesn't want anyone to practice our faith. He hasn't said this publicly, but we have heard that meetings have been stopped and services stopped. We are going to continue them here, but in secret, in the woods. It means we can't say anything about it to anyone, it mustn't be discussed. Otherwise we will all be in danger."

Nanni had never looked so scared before. "Hey, don't be frightened. I'll be with you and go wherever you go," Rija said, putting her arm around her sister hoping to give her some comfort. "Why don't you go back upstairs, and you can read some stories to me while you have breakfast in bed," suggested Rija. Nanni smiled, giving her sister a big hug before heading upstairs to her room.

Once Nanni was gone, Rija bore some tears. Her mother quickly sat beside her and held her as she had held Nanni. "Why is this happening Mother? Why doesn't anyone stop it? Why doesn't Aurelia stop it? Why doesn't Jei stop it?" She asked as frustration and anger grew.

Her mother calmed her down, pulling her daughter's head under hers. "Do you remember the story from the Amel Cristea of the prophet Anani?" Olyssia whispered. "He had a revelation from Jei and he sought to show love to all. He gave food to the hungry, he gave shelter to the homeless and he gave a family to the orphan. But there were still those who didn't like what he was doing. He suffered immensely from those who mocked him and beat him. But he knew what he was doing was right. Each day he would pray: 'Drythen, Jei, such pain afflicts me, such hurt seeks to destroy me. Yet I will not falter, for as long as I have breath, I will seek the will that is meant for me, in my suffering, you will guide me. In my weakness, you strengthen me. Until the day that I am called. Let my path be always righteous.' There are people and beings that have a twisted mind and look to harm others no matter who or what they are. That is the choice they have made. We just must make sure we choose our way, and don't let anything or anyone tear you from that path, no matter what happens to you. Remember those words. And remember love is always more powerful and far greater than any hate anyone can throw at you."

Olyssia stood up and went over to the cooker placing some of the sweet-smelling breakfast on a plate. She handed it to Rija. "Go on, your sister will be waiting."

Later that day, Philip went outside. The rain had eased but the wind was still blustery and cold. Normally this weather would keep him indoors, but he felt that he needed to get out and away from all that was going on.

Venturing to the woods where some of the villagers were now walking back from a prayer meeting, Philip went to find the tallest tree, the one that could be seen at the heart of the village.

To get onto the first branch required a high jump and then to pull himself up; this was the hardest part of the climb. Watching his every step and carefully navigating his way through the branches, Philip climbed.

The wind was rocking the tree which made it more difficult than normal, but he was determined to conquer it, even more so in the treacherous conditions. There were times he needed to grab a firm hold of the branch he was clinging on to, just to make sure the wind didn't blow him out of the tree. While the wind was cold, it felt fresh on his skin. He felt his short jacket sway in the breeze as the wind found its way up his blue trousers and yellow T-shirt.

He closed his eyes as he was halfway up and felt the tree go from side to side as the wind pushed it. He imagined that he was flying through the Dorian system and into the Gang of Saltus on the bridge of his own ship. There he stayed for a while, dreaming.

When at last his eyes opened, it was to the sound of shouting. He looked up and towards the village. Through the branches he could just make out the village hall and a few people that were there. He recognised Mandel instantly, but other beings were there in blue and grey combat uniforms with grey helmets and visors on. They were also heavily armed.

Philip thought it best he should stay in the tree for now, fighting off an inner battle to get down and get to his house. He assumed they were the Ranian troops. He had never seen them up close, or in person, only on the holographic image. With their visors on there was nothing to distinguish whether they were Aurelian or Ranian, both had similar figures, but he knew the skin was different.

A third soldier walked out of the Village Hall with a large silver container that the soldier pulled behind. Philip didn't see where the soldier went, he presumed they had a transport vehicle here somewhere. Philip finally recognised one of the others with Mandel: it was one of Rija's friends, Tyra, who had her legerteam the day it was announced Rana was coming. Her blonde hair was blowing as wildly in the wind, as wildly as the tree Philip was in. Still he watched.

The wind was blowing their voices towards him, and he heard the young woman shout: "YOU CAN'T TAKE OUR FOOD! WHAT WILL WE LIVE ON?!" She screamed and screamed: "HOW COULD YOU?! HOW COULD YOU?!" She seemed to charge towards the soldiers only for Mandel to hold her back. The troops' laughter carried in the wind and their mocking was scornful. Still, they took the container now full of food.

Mandel's grip loosened hoping she had calmed down. Mandel kept trying to reassure her, now others heard the commotion and stepped outside to help calm her down. But she fought her way out and charged towards the soldiers. Her figure vanished where Philip couldn't see, at least not from where he was, had he gone much higher, he would have been able to see everything.

A gasp of breath took him at the frightening sound of a gunshot and then a second. Now trembling, Philip clung to the tree tighter than anything. Watching the villagers rush to where she had gone. Philip hoped she was ok. Her and Rija were close friends and if anything happened to her, Rija would be devastated.

Minutes had gone by and the whole village was outside with the wind beating against them all. Wailing screams of tears and hurt he heard even from where he was. With every power of his imagination, he tried to wish the thoughts of Tyra away, but he couldn't. He mumbled to himself "take her home." Looking to the clouds, he mumbled it again: "take her home. Let her rest now. May we see through these dark days."

The tree was a comfort to him, it was his safe place. Eventually, he climbed down and made his way back home. His father greeted him with a solemn look. "Tyra was shot dead today because she attacked one of the Ranian soldiers. They warned us against any other uprising."

It was what Philip had hoped would never happen, it was the realisation that struck him. "But she didn't even have a gun, or any weapon!" Philip questioned. The injustice of it was burning inside him.

"I know," Dayala said softly, holding his son, "it's not fair. It's not right."

Evening came and night fell. Olyssia led Rija, Philip and Nanni to the woods with others from the village. At the centre of the wood, half the village gathered. Dayala was already there. Everyone had spread out with a couple of people keeping watch. Dayala started reading:

*"Then I saw from the ashes a new city rise up from the sun's burning rays. The city was made of pure gold where the descendant, who was like a mighty bird, but also a humble one, that changed from its hunting ways to reign. There it sat on the throne, and began a glorious reign over the stars and land; its name given was, 'peace.' For all those who read these words, this dark time will challenge all those who keep faith in Jei. The time will pass, peace will reign for a time and time again. Jei is the author of all, the one who will right the wrongs of those who seek to destroy."*

"Hold onto these words," Dayala continued. "This is part of a prophecy written over a thousand sun's orbits ago. It tells us of a Great War that will happen when great powers rise and fall. It tells that there will be great suffering. But what we need to hold onto is this: For all those who read these words, this dark time will challenge all those who keep faith in Jei. The time will pass, peace will reign for a time and time again. Jei is the author of all, the one who will right the wrongs of those who seek to destroy.

"This is the hope we must hold onto. I believe we are at the start of a long night; no one knows how long the night will last. But at the end of it, a new day will rise and a peace like no other."

"Through everything we go through, hold onto this hope, it will not last. Some will be called home when they can no longer fight, others will go on. Hold onto this hope." Dayala started praying with the rest of the gathered villagers following him. It lasted long into the night.

Philip went deep into thought after listening to many of the prayers. He thought about how he would put things right, how he would bring an army to Lepans and set everyone free. But then changed to how he would try and help people escape the turmoil. He looked over to his mother, her eyes were open with her demeanour looking troubled. Eventually she closed her eyes and faced the sky.

After the meeting, the villagers were told to walk back one by one to hide what had been going on. By the time he got back to his house, Rija and Nanni were already there, sitting at the kitchen table. Nanni cuddled her Hengest. Philip sat down with them.

It was a good few minutes before their parents walked back in. "Children, we have to prepare," Dayala said. "You will all need to have a bag packed in case Ranian troops come along and force us out." "We have also been thinking. If anything should happen to your father or I, it's important that you three try and stay together. We have heard there are people in Landburness who are helping children escape. If the situation we are in gets worse, that is what we may look at trying," Olyssia said. "We want you all to be safe. It is not safe for you here. Even less so if…"

Dayala went to hold and hug his wife. "It's going to get difficult. And we don't want you to suffer here. Promise us if anything happens you will find these people, they go by the name of George and Tabatha. Find them, and if Jei is willing, you will escape this. Now go pack a bag, keep it light. We never know when we might need it."

Philip's eyes lit up at the sound of the names wondering if it was the same couple, he had met that one time on Rana's victory day. The thought that it was them gave him comfort that it was people he had met and knew to be kind.

In all their eyes they saw a hurt building up. "Do not fear," Dayala said to them gently. "You are never alone, remember that. 'As the day turns to night and the night turns to day, your love is never torn from me. Everywhere I go you are always by my side, there is nowhere I can go, from you I cannot hide.' Always remember that."

Rija got up and took a number of hurried footsteps towards her parents embracing like she had never embraced them before. Philip and Nanni copied her. Nanni tried to wrap her arms around everyone. Her cries became the loudest. Rija and Olyssia knelt to cuddle her.

"I don't want to lose anyone," Nanni said helplessly.

"We'll always be together, you and I," Rija said to comfort her sister, "I won't leave you.

Besides, who else is going to do my hair?" She jested. The smile on Nanni's face was all that they wanted to see. Dayala and Philip embraced everyone. They held their huddle for as long as they could. Nanni loved it and wanted to remember this feeling for as long as she could.

"Go on," Dayala said softly. "Your mother and I Love you very much, and…" Dayala stopped himself before he broke down. He had never cried in front of his children before and didn't want them to see him that way.

The children went upstairs. At the top of the stairs before going into their separate rooms, Rija turned to her siblings. Philip could tell she was trying not to cry, her voice was brittle trying to hold it all back. "If anything happens, we must stay together, ok. We will leave Lepans together." She knelt to Nanni. Her hand went through her little sister's hair. "I promise you I won't leave you. Not if I can help it. Ok." Nanni threw herself onto her sister with her arms around Rija's neck.

"I love you." She whispered softly

# Chapter V

GEORGE RUSHED INTO THE bomb site of a room, being careful not to make it obvious to those across the street. He crouched down kneeling on the floor peering over the window frame. "She's there!" Philip whispered excitedly. "Nanni! I saw her... she's there!"

"Are you sure it's her?" George questioned.

"I only saw part of her face. But I know it's her," assured Philip, "we need to go and get her!" Philip was overcome with excitement. Imagination was one of his strengths, so often he went into his own world and thought up many scenarios, each one involved him in some different life and context, but right now, it was the idea that he could leave Lepans with Nanni and Rija.

"There is no easy way to get in there," George said.

Cody had sneaked in behind them both and had overheard the conversation. "The little girls do the chores around the place, she will be out to that bin again, I'm sure, probably towards the end of the night."

"What if I hid behind the bin? I could speak to her then, or at least speak to any of the other girls who are there." Philip was excited. He was jumping at every thought that crossed his mind hoping that one idea would work. It was taking every bit of will power to stop himself from walking into the bar to try and get to them.

"You won't be able to go until it's dark," George said, "even then, you will have to be careful no one sees you from the bar crossing the road. Even in the dark they are likely to see you. You will have to stay in the shadows to avoid being seen."

It was an agonising wait. Philip sat there in the cold room, peering regularly to see what was happening over at the bar. Night just wouldn't come quick enough for him. It seemed to go slower than the day breaking in. With one eye on the bar and another on the skyline, looking, straining for the lights of the windows to announce the night in.

Sky of bright blue slowly turned darker. At least two more times he had now seen this girl come out to the bins. A couple of times Philip thought it was time to make his move but was pulled back by George who told him it was still too early. Frustration grew as shadows from the buildings cast a darkness, still it was too light to make a move. Philip continued to wait.

A whole new crowd of Ranian troops appeared. Six or seven of them walking like a street gang who owned this part of the city, proudly strode confidently into the bar. Without any warning, Philip made a dash for it out of the wrecked door and over the darkened road. No being was outside on the benches, and to Philip's luck, no one else was walking by.

George and Cody had watched, agonisingly unable to stop him and hoped he would make it, but half expecting him to be caught. They watched his eager figure turn from light into shadow and vanish into the night of the small courtyard.

Philip crept treading on unseen glass and waste. Some crunched under his feet, others seemed soft, engulfing round his foot. The dark hid the black container of waste, but Philip remembered where they were after staring at them and the bar the whole day.

His hand was held out in front of him trying to feel his way towards them. The containers were made of a solid manufactured material, not as strong and warmer than metal. Philip eased it out, stepping on the waste that had fallen around it. After easing it out, he slid behind it, sitting himself down on the dirty floor and waited.

The smell was disgusting, the waste had been here for over a full suns' orbit and was almost unbearable. But Philip was determined to stick it out and wait as long as he needed to until the girl came out. Music was louder and clearer where he waited, he could see through the windows. The bar was bustling with Ranian troops with cig smoke filling the room and creating a large mist. Moans and groans, along with screams of passion were clearer as well; Philip wondered what was going on, but remembered what George had said, 'you wouldn't want to know.'

Other workers of the bar came out, some Ranians, other times it was young girls, each one was dumping more waste cramming it into the bin; none who came out was the girl he was after.

More Ranians had come and gone since he had staked his place behind the waste container. Their talk was of what they had got up to in the bar. They spoke of girls they had talked to, but it was unclear about what they were saying about them.

The back door that was next to where Philip hid flew open from the inside. Out came the girl carrying rags of sorts. Philip watched her open the waste container and place the rags on top of everything else in there. "Nanni…Nanni?" Philip whispered, trying to grab her attention. "Nanni…" he whispered again.

"Who's there?" A timid voice of a young girl replied. "How do you know me?" There was much fear in her high voice. Philip had never heard her so scared. He peered around a little more to make sure it was his little sister. The same puffy cheeks were presented to him along with their father's sterling grey eyes.

"Nanni…it's me, Philip. Your brother." Philip crept out from behind the black container, the darkness still camouflaging him. He saw his sisters' eyes light up in delight at seeing him, but there was a nervous anxiety now forming on her demeanour.

"Philip! You're alive! We thought the Ranian troops had found you and killed you. You can't get caught here, they will kill you for sure," she said hurriedly.

"Nanni, where's Rija? Is she with you?" Philip asked, keeping an ear and eye on the back door of the bar.

"She's in here," Nanni replied. "I hear Ranian soldiers being mean to her all the time. They lock her up in a room and hear horrible things going on, but I'm never allowed to see. Until afterwards when they tell me to go in and clean up. That's when I see Rija crying and curled up in bed. I try to help her, but she tells me to go away."

"I'm here to get you both out," Philip said. "I met someone who said they can get us away from Lepans. Do you remember, those people Mother and Father said? I found them. He is over the road in that burnt-out house."

"She won't listen to me," Nanni said. "We have barely spoken since we arrived here."

"Can you sneak me in?" Philip asked. "I can try and speak to her. I want us all to leave together."

"I'll try," Nanni said nervously, looking back at the door. "But it will have to be later tonight. The halls will be clearer. I'll find you here later. Go, before you are seen," Nanni said. She held out her hand for Philip to hold, then pulled it away and headed back into the bar.

Philip took care and stealthily headed back over the street to the house, sneaking in, no-one from the bar saw him. "Did you find them? Did you see her?" George asked hastily. His eyes beamed with anticipation, the prospect of saving even just one person from Lepans lifted his spirit.

"Yes, I did. She is going to try and sneak me into see Rija. Rija is not doing very well. The Ranians have been hurting her, every night since they arrived. I want to get them both out."

"We don't have much time," George said. Philip's eyes became confused. "Sago is leaving by the end of the day tomorrow. If you are to leave, you need to be on that ship tomorrow otherwise you will have to wait weeks, if not longer."

The young man became a face of determination. Instantly Philip put his hood up and headed back over when no one was watching or walking to or from the bar; he hid in the same place and waited.

He heard rooms above him and around him fade from one scream or groan to another.

Soldiers left the bar walking past unawares of the Aurelian lurking in the shadow. By his count a vast number had left the bar. Philip looked into the window for more clarification: all he saw was mist from the cig smoke, still a few bodies remained, and the music still hammered on.

The back door was opened slightly. Philip started to nudge his way out. "She was... amazing!" A gravelly voice spoke. Philip dived back behind the waste container knocking it against the wall. "What's that?" He looked up and saw the figures of Ranian soldiers now staring at his position. Philip crouched low down edging himself to a darker shadow. The steps came nearer. "I probably just knocked it when I opened the door," he said. Philip was relieved, releasing a huge breath of air.

Another hour or so went by, still Nanni had not appeared. Night was well and truly in. The early hours of the morning were approaching. The door opened again. This time Philip took more precautions and waited to see if it was his little sister.

"Philip...? Are you there?" Philip stepped forward. "Don't make a sound. There is hardly anyone about. The owner has gone for some rest, so we can sneak about more." She took his hand and led him in.

The first room was a kitchen that had smelled of all kinds of food, some meat, other root crops. None of it gave any appetite to a very hungry young Aurelian, his only focus was getting his sisters.

Nanni led him into a hallway which then led to a corridor and stairs. Both walked along the soft carpet of gold diamonds, crowns, and spades on a green background. Parts of it were frayed and worn. They passed door after door, each one was wooden, many had dents or marks in them. The corridor was narrow with the brown walls and a beige ceiling, making the space enclose around them.

Behind a number of the doors, the moans and screams continued, while others were silent. From what Nanni had said earlier about what goes on, they were more like a gateway to a graveyard as Philip passed them.

Sneaking slowly through the corridor being wary of any doors that could open suddenly, Nanni kept her eye on the way ahead, while Philip kept an eye behind. From what he had seen of the outside structure, they had walked through the L shape of the building and now were at the back.

"It's here." Nanni said softly. She gave a gentle tap with her knuckles. "Rija...it's Nanni...can I come in?"

No answer was heard. Nanni gently turned the handle and pushed the door open. It gave a slight squeal which made Philip double check around them for anyone coming. Nanni stuck her head around the door. All she saw was the slender figure of a girl, her back facing the door curled up covered only by the sheets of the bed. Her ivory legs were loosely hanging out of the sheets, the only flesh on show.

Holding Philip's hand, Nanni crept in, Philip closed the door behind them making sure not to make a noise. This was the first time Philip had seen Rija since she had been taken. As he looked at her lying on the bed, he barely recognised her. Already he noticed bruising on her legs. He started to feel hurt and pain for the suffering his sister had endured and wished he could have stopped it. Helpless he felt, hoping his arrival might spur her up from the grave-like pose she had adopted, but there was nothing.

"Rija…it's Nanni," she said softly and innocently, creeping quietly around the bed. "Philip has come. He says he can get us off Lepans and out of here. Rija… will you talk to me? Please, I don't like it when you don't talk to me. It's scaring me." Nanni pleaded. Her sweet voice became brittle very quickly. Philip hoped it wouldn't attract any attention.

Philip moved himself around the other side of the bed to try and see if he could make sure she wasn't asleep. "Rija, it's Philip. I have someone who says they can get us out of here and fly us to Aurelia. We can start a new life there. Someone can look after us. Rija, talk to us."

He peered over at her face. While he still saw the beauty that his parents and Nanni saw, her face was bruised, almost black and blue. Philip didn't want to react. As he looked closer, there were cuts that had scabbed over all the way from her face to just around her neck.

It was the look in her eyes that hurt him the most. Pure hazel, like a rich ring of gold or the birds eye view of the brown mountains, a two day walk from the village. They once had so much joy and laughter. He remembered his parents so gleeful, but at the same time, sad, at the sight of their eldest happy and almost grown up. He had stood by them as they watched her become a woman, saying how much they wished to see her as a little girl again, and go through all the turmoil and trials she put them through. As they looked on her then, it was all worth it.

Now Philip looked in her eyes and only saw an emptiness, like there was nothing in there, all that was left was a body for these soldiers to use as they pleased. Philip went to put his hand on her arm. He saw where it was under the covers and moved his hand slowly towards her. As his hand touches her skin, Rija jerked it back, in turn frightening Nanni and Philip.

"Go away!" Rija said. Like the rest of her, even her voice was unrecognisable to him. It was uncharacteristically pained. "Just go!" She said again. "I can't go with you. You will have to go alone!"

Nanni burst into tears. Philip tried to console her. He gave her a tight squeeze assuring her that he would try and talk sense into their big sister.

"Rija, look at you. You can't stay here. These people will kill you. We need you! Mother and Father aren't here to look after us. We need you! We need each other. Please, Rija," Philip said, almost begging.

His eyes kept falling on Nanni, seeing tears rolling down her face.

"Maybe I deserve to die, for what I am now!" Responded Rija.

Philip had no idea what to say. He was reminded of their father's favourite passage of the Amel Cristea: he spoke it out loud: "When those around me hurt and mock me, you are the shield that protects me. Even when I turn away, you are always waiting for me. You long to hold me and you never stop loving me, the darkest night can't hide your light. As the day turns to night and the night turns to day, your love is never torn from me. Everywhere I go you are always by my side, there is nowhere I can go, from you I cannot hide."

The words struck her. Like her father spoke to her, tears were shed, but still, she didn't move. Faintly, like a breeze in the air, a voice sang: it was clear yet still. There was no way to discern where it was coming from, or if it was a man or woman singing. But it was like the trickle of a stream close by that somehow surrounded him, yet he couldn't see it. The words were unfamiliar to Philip, but he heard them clearly: *Thfhuish thfhulu thfimulu yuluthf thflo kalomule.* Slowly the voice sang with a haunting yet sweet melody.

It dropped to the background as a gruff voice from the corridor was heard. It was talking to another man, if not two. "We have a girl just right for you," the voice said, "captured from a village out in the sticks. She was a pure one. Not anymore," the voice laughed. Philip and Nanni panicked, now fearing they might get caught as well as fear for their sister.

"Rija! We must go. Please come with us!" Philip begged again hoping that one more time might convince her.

"You need to go. If they catch you. They will kill you. Besides, I don't want you to see what they do to me," Rija said blankly.

"Rija! Rija! I'm not leaving you!" Nanni cried out.

Rija cried. "I love you. I'm sorry." She sniffed and closed her eyes. Philip took out of his pocket the piece of scripture that his father had given him and slipped it under her pillow. He grabbed Nanni's hand and dragged her streaming with tears to the window. He pulled the net to one side and saw that it wouldn't open. He grabbed a wooden chair that was by the other wall, he threw it with as much force and strength that he could muster.

The window shattered, spreading glass everywhere. Philip looked out and saw a shed below.

He turned back to Rija still with Nanni clutching his hand. "We love you. I will find you again. I promise."

Philip climbed out of the window perching his feet tenderly on the ledge. Nanni watched horrified that he might slip and fall. Composed and calculated, Philip looked at it as if he was jumping down from a tree to the ground, the height was around the same distance, except there was a possibility of rolling off the shed roof and then tumbling to the floor; he tried not to dwell on that too much.

Slightly bending his legs and springing himself up, Philip let go of the ledge landing down flat footed on the shed roof. There was a little stumble, but he managed to compose himself again standing upright. He turned back to the window and held his arms out towards Nanni. "Quick! Jump! I'll catch you," he whispered loud enough for her to hear. The door to the bedroom knocked. Nanni saw Rija jump up bolt upright with so much fear on her face it made Nanni even more scared. It started to open, Nanni fixed her eyes on her brother and burst into tears again, then jumped. Philip caught her and stabilised his feet managing not to fall off the roof.

Philip climbed down, then encouraged Nanni to jump into his arms. To their left as they faced the back of the bar, there was a beaten old fence. Philip instantly made his way for it, pulling Nanni along with him. It led out into a tight path between the bar and another concrete house and then back out into the street.

Outside the bar was quiet, but voices echoing down the street kept Philip and Nanni from heading back to the house. The voices went into the bar, six of them Philip thought. Once they had disappeared, he led Nanni over to the house where George Lawson Quinn and Cody Filema were waiting.

Inside the two adults waited and were surprised to only see Nanni come out with Philip.

"What happened?" George asked. His eyes widened as if a dread had filled him.

"I couldn't convince Rija to come," Philip said helplessly. "She just lay on the bed crying. She was covered in bruises. I think they have been hurting her." He found himself at the point of breaking down. The hope he had of reuniting with his two sisters had driven him this far. But now he felt like a failure and that he was somehow letting his family down.

Cody moved towards him, her arm extended placing it affectionately on Philip's shoulder.

"Your sister has been hurt badly. She probably doesn't even recognise herself. It's the cruelty of this place," she said with a malicious eye piercing the bar across the street. "If you want to help your sister, then help her by getting off Lepans."

"Cody is right," George interjected, "if you want to save Rija, then you have to leave Lepans tomorrow. Tell Aurelia your story. Tell them what is happening here. If they knew, word would get back to the High King and he will want to retake the planet. But you must leave on that transport tomorrow night, you, and your sister." George looked out at the night.

"Morning we be upon us soon and our ability to head through the streets difficult. We have a rendezvous to make with my wife and the others." George knelt to Nanni. "I've heard much about you. We are going to get you off Lepans. It will be a dangerous journey. Stay with your brother at all times." He stood back up towering over her and glanced again at the open sky and the horizon where the line of the morning would appear. "Cody has managed to gather us food. We need to leave now!"

# Chapter VI

THE BEAT THUMPED STILL, a little louder than it was before, George thought, as it bounced off all the buildings in the street. The air was still and mischievous like a ghostly part of the town where spirits spied on those that walked alone.

George moved quickly, almost in a hurry to get away from the bar. The beat faded slowly into nothing. Philip and Nanni followed behind with Cody holding up the rear. George's eyes were wary of all that was going on around them. Soon they would enter the inner city, the known hunting ground for Ranian troops looking for an Aurelian kill.

They had taken a different route from the way George had taken Philip to the bar, the buildings were different for a start: instead of architectural wonders built of either the beige stone of Aurelia or the cloudy stone, commonly used throughout Lepans, they were simpler designs, more efficient with space and very square. They looked like offices rather than any kind of shop or factory. For a moment as they passed the buildings, Philip half wondered in a slight daze what happened in the buildings, what business was being run in there? Had the Ranians brought over their businesses when they started to colonise, or did they just take over the Aurelian's businesses.

He was snapped out of it by a slight cry from his little sister. Philip looked down and saw a grave face with her bottom lip poured slightly in a sulk. "I want Rija," she mumbled quietly, almost under her breath but loud enough so that her brother could hear, "I miss her."

Philip crouched down in front of her, checking all around them, his eyes warmed, grateful to see her cute face, but it pained him to see her so unhappy. "Hey!" He said sympathetically, his heart almost melted at her, right there and then all he wanted to do was give her the biggest cuddle he could; since he had found her again, there hadn't been the time. "Rija is unwell, and she needs help…" he said trying to think of the right words to say as he didn't want to upset Nanni anymore. "You and I, we need to help her by getting help to come here. We need to tell Aurelia what is happening here.

"Then we can try and help Rija." He gave her a warm embrace, a short lived one but still a loving one between a brother and his younger sister. "I promise you, we won't forget her. We will find her again."

Philip stood up again and hurried his pace behind George with Nanni being dragged along afterwards. Shadow had become hard to come by in this part of the city: the lights of the lamps were bright white spots from up high, even the glass structures either side of them had bright lights high up that lit up the street. Drones of hovering vehicles surrounded them like phantoms watching their prey.

Hurriedly the group were almost running light footed through the streets. There was no hiding place to take cover in. George veiled a worried concern in his demeanour. Should any Ranian patrols catch them here, they would be executed on the spot.

Buildings of glass and cloudy stone were the pinnacle of the city business centre. In a matter of hours these streets would be rife with Ranian citizens, the new occupants of Lepans. A menacing drone became louder. Accompanying the drone Philip could hear a different sound, a familiar one: it was like what he had heard back in the bar when he was with Rija. *Thfhuish thfhulu thfimulu yuluthf thflo kalomule.* It was a language he had not heard before. He found himself drawn to it, almost letting go of Nanni's hand. He found himself wandering off, George shouted to him to come back, in truth he himself was clueless as to what to do. He started following the young man, constantly trying to call him back. Each time Philip just gave this response: "can't you hear it? It's coming from here I think," he said as his curiosity was leading his footsteps. He went past a fountain with lights shining up through the water pool surrounded by pattern tiles carefully placed together. The flowing water perfectly accompanied the song Philip could hear; he then felt a warm breeze touch his face. Each time he lost it, he would turn to find it. He felt a warmth on the breeze brush against his face. He turned and the breeze was gone, then would turn to find it again. It was like it was calling him with the song being carried on the breeze.

In truth the song was always in front of him, but at the same time, always around him.

All now followed him curious to know where he was going. Passing different restaurants and clubs all closed for business, while hovering drones continued to get louder, like they were picking up on the Aurelian's scent.

More buildings built for executives and leading businesses, neatly laid alongside one another, all passed by. Lights still lit their path, but now they were getting few and far between as spotlights in the paving stones now lit the night, guiding the Aurelians through the deserted streets.

Each new street entered, and corner turned, the breeze became warmer on Philip's face and the song became clearer; still the same words of an ancient language, left behind long ago in another time by another people.

Light became shadow, the path Philip chose was darkness, the black alley of two old factories.. All continued to follow. Philip again felt the warmth in the breeze with the song faintly carried on it, like a whisper that came and went.

The narrow path opened out into a square. In the centre was an old temple built of Aurelia's beige stone, now turned a shade greyer, though it had not the richness or majesty of the other temples Aurelia had built, the stones were stained, damaged from the elements of Lepans environment. There was a spiral that reached high into the sky, once it would have been the tallest building in that area of the city, now it was overshadowed by all the other buildings built after its time. What windows were left had turned cloudy or a brown, a sign of neglect from the community the temple once served.

At the foot of the tower where the steeple crowned the once great structure, two large wooden doors with thick beams heading across and up the door like a large grid. It was heavy to open. Philip was assisted by George as the two grabbed the iron handle and pushed the door open. It was stiff and heavy to move. As momentum took it, the weight suddenly pulled their arms dragging them into the building.

A great darkness filled the void, a darkness that was blacker than the night outside, as the daylight was on the verge of bursting forth.

The four of them crept in not knowing what was inside. Suddenly a light like a torch flashed in their eyes. Silhouettes of figures approached. With the torch light on their eyes, the light blinded them. A voice called out: "George...George is that you?" It was a softly spoken voice with a sweet tone.

George's face dropped in amazement, "Tabatha... Tabatha..." George became excited and quickened his step to embrace his wife. "How come you are here? We were supposed to meet in the underground by the port," George said with wonder.

"Ranian patrols had increased. We were on our way to the underground, but to keep out of sight from the patrols, we were forced to change our direction. We found ourselves here. How did you find us?" Tabatha asked.

Tabatha had flicked her torch to briefly show the others with her. In the glimpse, no more than a few blinks of the eye, it was enough for George to see children, at least seven young girls and boys not far off the same age as Nanni and Philip, some older, some younger. All were either orphans or have been encouraged by their parents to leave Lepans. It was that moment of light that highlighted how deprived these children had been in the last year. Clothes were worn and torn, skin had not seen clean water for months and only scraps of food had been rationed and consumed for days if not longer.

"It was Philip here. He just seemed to know the way," replied George, throwing his arm around Philip's shoulder.

"I heard a song. I thought it might be you singing," Philip said.

"No we have been here in silence hoping Ranian patrols didn't find us. What was the song?" Tabatha asked. Before Philip could answer, Tabatha found herself feeling a little rude. "Please, I'm sorry. You must come and sit down. You look like you have been up most of the night."

Philip sat down on an old pew that was in the temple. He watched as George introduced Cody to his wife. The exchange was probably telling Tabatha about what had happened to them. Tabatha then came to sit by him bearing a drink. The torch light showed Philip more of her appearance: she had sunflower blonde hair and brown eyes that gave a look of warmth at Philip, it was as if his own parents were looking lovingly at him.

She handed him a hot drink in the lid of a flask: it had a sweet taste with a very slight bitter aftertaste. Phillip felt there was a kindness about her that naturally permeated through her. As morning light began to drown out the darkness of the temple, a faint dark blue in the sky started to give light to the city surrounding them. Philip was now able to see Tabatha fully, her white vest top and dark blue synthetic cotton trousers had stained with dust and dirt. Brown flat sole jelly shoes looked as if they had walked across the planet with signs of wear showing on the sides.

"George told me what happened with your older sister. I'm sorry. She has been hurt, changed because of what she has been through. She no longer sees herself as how you might see her. You have to look after Nanni now, you are all she has." She placed her hand gently on Philip's. "We will keep an eye on your sister. If we can, we will get her out. But it may take time."

Philip smiled softly at her. He sighed and stared at the other children gathered in the temple, many of them were lying down with each other's laps as pillows trying to get some much-needed rest. "Do you miss your son?" He asked curiously.

"Every day," Tabatha said. Her smile looked forced. Behind it, Philip saw a regret, a pain instilled in her eyes. "We wanted to take him with us. But life out there, as you have witnessed, is not something you would wish on any child, especially your own." She looked fondly at Philip.

"You remind me of him, you know. John had, and still has an adventurous spirit. He always loved spaceships. His Grandfather, George's father, is Admiral of the Aurelian fleet. We thought it best he stayed there with him.

"Where is he now?" Philip enquired.

"Where we thought he would be. When he was young, he played game after game, imagining himself as Admiral of the fleet. As soon as he went to stay with his Grandfather, we knew it was only a matter of time before he joined. Now he is serving under Captain Will Leod of the Sun of War Eversor. I'm pretty sure that when he can, he will be Captain of his own ship. He has that drive in him."

"When did you speak to him last?" Asked Philip. "Just before the invasion was the last time we spoke.

Even then, he was more interested in his own life in the fleet. His answers were short and vague. When he first joined and we spoke, he was so excited about his first fews days and weeks on the Eversor. As the next few years carried on, teenage attitudes came in. It was like he became less interested in us. You can understand it…" Tabatha said sighing, "we had been so distant, and not seeing him in so long, you can understand it. It's our one regret. We loved our job and our mission on Diasos, we always wished we could have spent more time with our son. Sometimes there is a cost to pay for a faith and life following Jei. Your parents knew that too well."

Both could now see the full decor of the temple: a moment captured in time and place, a faith, a deity worshiped. Symbols, paintings and carvings in wood and stone of old stories and passages from the Amel Cristea: Jei, the great being of light and love watching over the worlds. There were depictions of the three beasts and the symbol of peace- the cross arrow points of Jei.

Up on the ceiling, wooden boards separated the sky from the air inside the temple, holding them up, the wooden frams in a triangle. Every now and then specks of dust cascaded down from the rays, it could be seen in the emerging daylight rays. It all fell sprinkling on the Aurelians resting on the pews.

Since they had walked in, the air had smelt stale, even as the night passed and the day entered the unmistakable scent still lingered around them. Philip had got used to it by now. He had always wondered what the great city temples were like. His only experience was some full sun's orbits ago, when Minister Arcehad, Archbishop of the Faith to the High King, came to preach. Such a guest had not been in nearly a full twenty suns' orbit. Philip remembered much of the anticipation of it, the excitement in his parents' eyes lifted his own joy and his sisters', all were excited.

Then came the day, the family went in with many from the village. Everything Philip had been told about the Temple of Jei at the heart of the city centre was accurate: marvellous beige stones built as high as a four-storey building with arch windows to match the majesty, some even compared it to the Temple of Jei in Vortigern the capital of Aurelia, some said that it would never match to the grandness of that building. The overall event was generally underwhelming, at least for someone a couple of suns' orbits younger than Nanni it would be. Still the memory of that building stuck with Philip. About three months into Rana's occupation of Lepans, it was reported that the Temple of Jei was torn down, in its place the Anguis,

Rana's symbol of the coiled snake like a ring with its tail breaking into the middle of it.

"Why did Jei let this happen?" Philip questioned. He felt guilty about asking it, like it was showing a lack of faith, but he was genuinely curious. Up to the last few weeks he had never really contemplated such philosophical ideas.

Tabatha paused for thought. "I don't believe he wants them to happen: for one the scripture says we are given free will, to do as we please. This is a result of Rana's free will. Two, scripture says we are not, and never will be immune from the trials that life may throw at us. But instead, we have someone who is always there with us. Through whatever we go through, holding us and pulling and dragging us through. Like even if your boat sinks on the water, and you have a friend who helps you out, you still get wet, but your friend has stopped you from becoming overwhelmed by it all."

"By the sounds of things, you have been called to Jei. He seems to have blessed you with the gift of hearing," Tabatha said, changing the subject, "you heard a song that guided you here, right to the very building we were in. Jei is amazing, how he can do incredible things like that."

"What do you mean?" A puzzled brow appeared on the young man's head. A time and question like this was when his father would step in and read off some passage of scripture; that just made things even more confusing.

"People often ask, 'if Jei can speak, why can I never hear him?' My response is always: 'to hear Jei's voice would be like hearing the sound of creation, hearing the sound of perfection. How can our ears even translate, or even take that in? So, I believe that through thought, feeling, or instinct, as some might put it, Jei speaks to us. Or in your case he used a song.

"You see, people don't believe in miracles. They often claim that they are a collection of coincidences," Tabatha continued, "yet miracles are out there, it's like Jei is revealing a part of himself with everyone. It was a miracle for example that you found us here. You avoided detection from all the Ranian patrols, and then stumbled on the same building as we have. For me it says Jei is watching over us and helping us. I believe you will get to the transport ship in time tomorrow, and you will get to Aurelia." She smiled at Philip, giving him a fresh hope.

Nanni had nestled her way into Philip's lap as he had talked. Tabatha had given her a soft toy Hara to try and settle her. She embraced it as it was similar to the toy Hengest that was taken from her when she was taken captive from the village. With her finger and thumb, she rubbed the softness of the long ears, the smoothness of one side and the furry side of the other was addictive to keep playing with, soothing her thoughts. He looked down at her and stroked her amber hair. It was all knotted and tangled, he tried hard not to pull on it too much as to not wake her up.

"You must rest," Tabatha said as she stood up. "We have a long day ahead of us." Philip watched her head over to her husband and sat by him. His demeanour was of a contemplative one, sitting on a pew by himself. His head was in his hands as he leant over with his elbows on his knees.

Tabatha sat by him and gently stroked his back. He sat up and sighed. "You look troubled,"she said softly.

"I'm just worried we aren't going to make the ship tomorrow. Time is running out. How are we supposed to get there in broad daylight?" His voice was grave. He reached into his pocket to bring out a small book bound in a maroon leather, with thin pages, very fine to touch, any slight overzealous turn would rip the page clean through; the size of it meant it could fit perfectly in his one hand, and ideal for carrying around on his person.

He opened it up to take his mind off the situation facing them. After skim reading several passages George settled on a page:

*Doubt and anguish can destroy the very soul of a person. If the words within you tell you it is impossible, or that you can't do it, then it is you who is believing the lie within yourself. If we were to open ourselves up to the unimaginable, the very ideas we struggle to conceive, then and only then can you achieve your full potential. For Jei gave life, and with it, an abundance of love. It is that love that encourages us to find the very heart of our being and to use it to honour and serve Drythen, Condel Secan.*

"We've made it this far," Tabatha said, trying to bring her husband encouragement. Suddenly, her own complexion dropped a little. "What are we going to do? Are we going to try and leave, and make our way back to John?"

"He'll be too busy in the fleet to see us," George said in a jest.

"There are so many others who need help here, do we abandon them? And go back to the safety of Aurelia? It would certainly be easier." Tabatha rested her head on her husband's shoulder. Both sat silently in peace and watched the children in their care sleep. "Jei has led us here so far," George said. "Perhaps we shall see what he has prepared for us. If he wants us to leave, he will enable it. If he wants us to stay, then let his will be done." Tabatha took his hand and held it tightly.

"I suppose I should go and find a way to get us out of here and to the port in time," George said, sighing. He kissed his wife on the cheek and stood up. Tabatha wished him good luck and that she would pray for his safe return.

He lifted his hood back up over his head and headed for the door. Silently opening it and heading out into the day, staying close to the buildings and taking care to avoid any Ranian civilians that might sound the alarm.

The square was clearer to see, a road surrounded the green where the Temple had been built. Transport vehicles in many different shapes. Beige transport carriages from Aurelia were parked up while others were having their oval shape driven around the city joining the other hundreds and thousands of vehicles hovering around.

Wandering a little way across the green, unfamiliar streets were ahead, George went on warily. His eyes switched from looking for a means, an inspiration to help their cause, and any Ranians who might be looking at him suspiciously.

Most of the streets he could see ahead were either empty of Ranians, that he could see, or had only a handful of people in. George knew the city centre was to the south of his position. He looked north and headed for the street there.

On the street a larger beige carriage had stopped. Out of it came four Ranian males. Each one wearing long jackets that came down to just below their knees, all four jackets were a different colour; gold, midnight blue, a stone grey and Sangria red. All the outfits had matching or complementing waistcoat and trousers with a cravat added at the neck of a white shirt; each Ranian was an image of the fashion within the Jubal Galaxy.

The four men went cheerfully chatting away into a building of grey stone: it was fronted with a great glass sheet made up of six individual ones, what was inside, George couldn't see. What intrigued him was the beige carriage that was still hovering above the ground as if it was waiting. George moved in slowly, taking care with each step he took.

Another figure, a woman, got out. She wasn't Ranian. Instead, she looked more like a native of Diasos: the unmistakable monolid eyes and espresso skin were a familiar sight for George to see. Dressed in a white suit, the traditional garb for those in the domestic and commercial service industry, the woman headed into the building after the four Ranian men. By the time George had reached the carriage the woman had come out again. "Can I help you?" She asked with a strong accent. There was a little agitation in her voice, George thought. He kept his head down with the top of his hood covering his skin colour.

"Correct me if I'm wrong, but are you from Diasos?" George asked, hoping to gain her interest.

"Part of my family is. I'm from Kratia. Why do you ask?"

"Curiosity," George said. "My wife and I live on Diasos, I am an engineer for a company there. We were visiting friends when Rana invaded. I was hoping you might be able to help." George played his card and he knew it was a risky one. There was nothing to stop this woman from driving off and informing the patrols.

"You're not Ranian. You're Aurelian. I feel for you, believe me I do. Life here is becoming like it is in the Avian Republic. But if I get caught helping you, I get killed and so does my family; it's too risky."

"We are there because of those struggles in the Avian Republic. The engineering job I have is a front. Really, my wife and I are Missionaries, our desire is to help people. What brought you here?" George asked, hoping to find something that she could see the situation from his perspective.

"If you must know…I'm a refugee here. After my Father was killed in the riots, my Mother took us to the port paying the last of what money we had to get on any ship that would take us. We came here because of the prospect of working on an Aurelian colony, so starting a new life here seemed like a good idea."

"Then you of all people will know my problem," George said hurriedly with an eye on the building and a view up ahead of other Ranian citizens walking their way. "Please…let me show you something. If you decide to still leave and go about your day, fine. But don't just leave until you have seen what I have."

The carriage driver agreed and prompted George to get in. There he discovered her name was Sibyl Ayatama. The two briefly chatted as the carriage made its way to the Temple. It only took a few minutes, in that time George prayed and prayed for a miracle.

He kept a close eye on all that was around until he reached the door. He turned suddenly to Sibyl: "please you have to promise me, if you do choose to go, which is fine, but please don't report what you have seen." George walked her toward the temple where the others were waiting.

Sibyl nodded with curiosity glaring with her purple eyes. George opened the door and invited her in. Her face slunk and her jaw dropped at the sight of the children and young people that were gathered.

"We are trying to get these children off Lepans. They no longer have their parents. We can't let them stay here," George whispered to her. "There is a ship waiting for us at the port. It leaves at dark tonight. I have to get these children there. Please can you help?"

Sibyl bit her lip and was already regretting the words she could feel coming into her mouth: "Ok!" She said softly. There were images of her own mother begging others to help them. So many turned them down, but it was the kindness of one that made the difference. She found herself compelled to be that one who helped, to show the kindness that was shown to her and her mother.

"We will have to hurry!" She said. "Only load in two at a time, we can't have anyone see us." Sibyl warned. A gracious thanks was given by George and Tabatha; she even stretched to a hug, which surprised the carriage driver. Tabatha then went on to wake the children up and tell them to hurry up, and not to make a sound.

# Chapter VII

ᗡᗡᗡ

ALL THE CHILDREN LAY down on the grey bobbled steel floor, legs crossing over heads while George and Philip sat hooded on the soft cream leather seats one facing the front, the other facing the rear; Tabatha and Cody lay with the other children as the carriage started making its way through Landburness.

Just as the outside shell of the carriage was beige, so was the inside. Its shell was made of a combination of materials and chemicals all cooked together. The end product is a firm hard shell-like glass but not as fragile or easy to break. The front cabin where Sibyl Ayatama, the carriage driver sat, was compact with enough room for her chair, a passenger chair and the holographic controls. Each carriage was controlled and steered in a similar way to a Sun of War: the helm required both hands, fingers and feet delicately controlling velocity and pitch along with the steering.

The carriage passed through the city centre. With a side eye view, both George and Philip looked on the outside of the carriage: so many Ranians flooded the streets going about their daily business, all following the fashions of the Galaxy. George thought it was amazing how quickly the Ranians had adapted and evolved the society of Lepans in such a short space of time.

Philip saw all the buildings, once the pride of the Aurelian colony, now it was overrun by Aurelia's enemy, it was like thieves had robbed everyone's houses, throwing out all the owners and living in the houses themselves. All on the street ignored the journey of the carriage, blending into the background amongst all the hovering vehicles and carriages.

The port was on the northern side of the city. All in the carriage were far beyond uncomfortable by now. Ragged children wriggled and fidgeted with moans and groans about wanting to get out. Tabatha reassured them regularly that the journey would be over soon.

All were hungry, where their next scraps of food would come from, no one could tell. The port drew nearer. With every meter to mile that the carriage got closer, disquiet like a fever was building in Philip. He had seen enough to know that Aurelians, especially children, don't just walk into a port and escape on a trading ship. He had started to press George for some idea of what they would do. But in front of the other children, George remained behind a veil of secrecy with not wanting to worry any of the children.

The carriage arrived: great columns of white stone supported a triangular roof of the same white stone. Carved on the remains were letters that once read, Beorgan Healicnes Saloman *X High King of Aurelia*. In the year of Rana's occupation, they had been determined to remove those words from the great arch, with only a few ruined marks remaining, barely recognisable as words.

"We have a checkpoint!" Sibyl's voice shouted from the cabin. "We can't go through. We will be seen!" Her agitated voice did nothing for Philip's nerves. Now a cold was shivering down his spine and nowhere near dissipating.

"Turn around and head back to the entrance columns. Drop us off there. We can make our own way from there," George shouted. Philip looked at the face of Tabatha hoping she might persuade her husband from the idea. But none came. She held out her hand, which he grabbed and gave it a squeeze, mouthing words of affection and love to her.

The carriage pulled over to the lay-by in the entrance. Philip saw a large grated fence had been put up all around the port that had gone down to the checkpoint where they had turned around. It was a sure sign that Carne, the self-appointed Governor of Lepans, had no desire to see any Aurelians leave without proper punishment.

George, still with his hood up, got out of the carriage and disappeared towards a white building hidden within the columns. Philip watched him carefully. He saw George check vigorously everywhere, all around him, before he went into the building. In moments, he came back out bearing blankets of sorts and headed purposefully for the carriage.

He opened the door. "Right! Quickly now. Put this round you," he said to the two smallest children: they were at least three suns' orbits younger than Nanni. With fear and speed, they ran with the blanket over them and went straight into the building, George followed them.

Philip wondered if they were all going to be seen., after all, it was going to look suspicious, a carriage stopped, pulled over in the entrance arch of the port.

Fortunately, the roof was providing some cover, and the darkened clouds provided a dampened light, it meant there was a chance the Aurelians would all be hidden, if they were quick and didn't do anything to draw attention to themselves.

George came back, more of the children went undercover. It carried on until there was just Philip Nanni and Tabatha left. George went up to Sibyl: "thank you so much. May Jei bless you with many blessings and give you peace."

"Good luck missionary. May Jei be with you," she replied.

Philip had ushered Nanni out and quickly followed Tabatha with George hurriedly pacing behind still with an eye watching all around. As he approached the building, Philip wondered how everyone was going to fit. It was only slightly bigger than a hut and looked more like a storage room than anything.

He entered only to find no one was there. George quickly closed the door behind them.

Without saying any words, he launched himself to the ground gently ushering Nanni off an iron panel. After grabbing a long metal rod, something that looked like it had broken off a ship somewhere, he wedged it in a hole in the panel and started to lift the panel up. His teeth were gritted, but the panel came up.

"Get down there quickly," he said.

Tabatha went down first and helped Philip lower Nanni down. Philip was next, with George following soon after carefully lowering the panel back down. "What is this? How did you know about it?" Philip asked.

"When Rana defeated the Aurelian fleet, the workers here knew it wouldn't be long until they imposed themselves. Fearing, and preparing for the worst, the workers knew Rana would seal off the port to all Aurelians. So, they worked night and day to create this tunnel. We found out about it from a former worker who was spreading the word about it. We were in the village where we were staying. This man came into the village with nothing but his now ragged clothes and a backpack. All he said to us is, 'people are trying to leave, but Ranian troops are doing their best to stop them. I've come from the port at Landburness. We created a tunnel that Rana will never know about. In the old storage unit in the entrance columns, to the right as you enter. Go through it to the end and it will bring you up on the far side of the shipyard. It will bring you up into the old entrance kiosk for incoming pilots.' He told us to find a ship and leave. It took a while, but we made contact with Sago. Hopefully, he will be waiting for us there."

They walked and walked through the darkness, treading on dirt and wood with the soil up above being held up like it was a dark mine. A few lights had been scattered along the way to give a little guidance. Like the night walk through the city the previous night, each step was taken lightly. The damp of the soil was strong and the air thin: each breath was shorter than it normally was with traces of dirt flying into their mouths as they walked. Nanni hated it and was moaning, almost crying as quietly as she could, still clutching the soft Hara given to her by Tabatha.

Philip did his best to calm her, but she still called out for Rija.

Once they had reached the other storage room, George kept himself by the door while Tabatha kept all the children quiet and calm. She told them all, including Philip and Cody to take each other's hands and pray. The other children had closed their eyes, Philip looked at George and was curious to see what he was doing. He was peering with the metal door only open enough for his one eye to see into the shipyard.

Voices of security and crews from ships coming and going could be heard, conversation after conversation, none could be deterred what it was about, but was relieved when it wasn't about them.

Nanni had been disturbed from the prayer. She opened her eyes and looked at her brother with such sadness: "where's Rija? We can't leave without Rija," she whined. Philip bent down and hugged her, squeezing her tightly. The squeeze made her drop the Hara, but she was glad for the hug.

"We aren't leaving her. We are going to get help. We will find her again. But first we need to get off Lepans," Philip said to try and reassure her. It was all too much for the young girl. Her face went red with tears instantly falling from her sterling grey eyes. She sobbed wheezing with each breath she brought in. It started to panic a few other children, they themselves started to get a little tearful. Tabatha and Cody did their best to reassure them and got them back into praying. Philip softly hushed Nanni, soothing her as best he could with words of hope that they will get to see their sister again, they were the only words Philip could think of to ease his sister's unhappiness.

Hours must have passed by. The children had calmed and now waited patiently again for their next instructions. Philip went over to George. "What can you see?" He asked.

"I can see right across the yard. The ship we want is right on the far side. But I have seen no sign of Sago. Once I see him, I will go to him; it won't be long now."

Within a matter of minutes and without warning, George left the storage room. Philip took his place looking out the door. Across ahead of George's path, Philip saw a large ship like a giant ant, grey and battered bearing many scars of travelling across the Galaxy.

In front of the ship was a man, shorter than George dressed in a long leather jacket and black shirt and trousers. His hair was thin and grey receding on his forehead. The most distinguishing feature was his hawk nose, typical of the people of Candela in the Phrygian system.

George's hood was still up, it was like he was trying to disguise himself as a crew member of Sago's ship. It seemed to be working. Philip saw the two of them talking: it was very convincing, anyone who didn't know what was going on would have easily been fooled by the charade. George went into the ship with Sago. After a few minutes, coming down from the ramp under the belly of the ship, the two of them appeared again, this time wheeling a large black container, almost as big if not bigger than the bins that were outside the bar where Rija was kept captive. Both started to walk towards the storage room.

Guards in black and grey combat gear patrolled the area in pairs with the occasional eye glanced on the goods coming in and going. There was a hope that there was so much going on at the port with all the other ships, the Aurelians' escape would go unnoticed.

Sago and George kept wheeling the large container over. They stopped it outside the storage room door. Philip saw Sago stand in front of it. He then went off to talk with another crew, whilst keeping an eye on the container and the storage room.

George snuck back inside the storage room. "Quick! I need the young ones first. You must move quickly! Now come on. Hurry!" George went before them, opening the container doors that were situated on the long side of it. "You need to squeeze in closely. We need as many of you in as possible."

The others started cramming themselves in. Seven children were crammed in, five more were left. This included Philip and Nanni. Nanni had not wanted to leave her brother's side and was afraid of being crammed into the small space. The other three that were left were older children, two boys and a girl. Philip assumed they would pose as Sago's crew and walk on to the ship as normal. It was a risky plan, but Philip had no idea what else they could do. Another trip of bringing the box to and fro from the ship would attract attention, and risk getting caught. "The rest of you, come here," George's voice said quietly.

Philip went out telling Nanni to stay with Tabatha. "I want to go with you," Nanni whined. Philip tried to calm her again, but she kept holding his hand tightly. "I want to go with you," she said adamantly.

"We don't want to get caught," Philip said, "stay with Tabatha. We will be leaving soon,"

Tabatha tried to gently pull her back repeating Philip's words. Nanni continued to whine a little, Philip had no choice, he had to go on.

The other three were already outside. "Tabatha... Cody...come out now," George whispered loud enough for them to hear. The two women walked out; Tabatha held Nanni's hand. "Try to stay on the other side of the container. Stay out of the view of the guards at all costs," instructed George. Slowly Philip along with the other three started pushing the container, while George led the way.

As he pushed, Philip took an occasional glance at what was going on around: there were all kinds of ships, most were grey of metal, others were white. It was difficult to see the full size and shape of them as he only had a moment to look, and the container, he pushed along the yard blocked much of his view, along with the light starting to drop into a bleak dusk.

Halfway across the yard, now almost fully exposed with no going back, Philip, along with the others, started feeling anxious and excited at the same time, though anxiety was winning the battle in the four of the youngsters who pushed. A bulky lad with ginger hair was next to him. Philip had no idea who he was, or where he came from. But the first impression was that he was a tough lad with his big exterior, destined to grow into a strong man. But it shocked Philip a little, the lad was shaking, quivering, his pasty white arms wouldn't stop shaking. Tears were running down his cheeks, which he did his best to hide.

Still, they pushed and pushed. They finally reached the ship. "Put your backs into it!" Sago could be heard shouting. Philip assumed he was trying to convince those around them they were the crew. They had almost got the container up and on a flat surface. There was much relief. They were on the ship with only the ramp to close.

"MY HARA!" Nanni shouted, before anyone could stop her, she ran down the ramp and back towards the storage hut.

"I'll go after her! Stay here!" Insisted George.

Philip began to panic, his heart was almost stopping and racing at the same time. He didn't want to shout for her, hoping the business of the personnel coming in and leaving would hide her presence there on the shipyard. George managed to catch up with her and held her tightly. He didn't bring her back, instead they kept on walking towards the storage room.

Both vanished inside with George keeping a careful eye around him. Seconds later both emerged, Nanni holding the grey ruffled Hara under her arm by its neck as tight as she could.

George hurried their steps.

"HEY! STOP!" A voice growled. Philip cast his eyes to his right, gazing toward the main building. Two guards now charged towards them. George clocked them and grabbed Nanni's hand, bolting the two of them toward the ship.

Gunshots were fired toward them. Philip's heart stopped. He shouted out: "NO! NANNI!"

She stopped running and stood still in the opening created on the concrete yard. His eyes widened to wonder why she had stopped, then he saw George Lawson Quinn pause, blood started pouring through his clothes before he fell to his knees.

"GEORGE!" Tabatha shouted. "Start bringing the door up," she ordered Sago, "leave as soon as the girl is on board." Sago nodded and started to close the ramp as slow as he could.

She bolted down the ramp and headed for Nanni who was in floods of tears and screaming her heart out, lost and with no idea what she should do. It only took seconds for Tabatha to arrive. One look towards the Ranian guards now charging themselves, guns drawn, prompted her to grab Nanni's hand and pull her along, only allowing herself a fleeting glimpse at her dead husband face down on the ground.

The ship drew near, as she ran, she picked Nanni up with all her strength, the Ranian guards ordering her to stop. Philip and Cody threw themselves on the edge of the closing ramp holding out their hands grabbing Nanni who was holding Hara tightly. She was pulled in quickly. Philip held his hand out for Tabatha. Two more gunshots were fired. Tabatha flinched back and forth twice as both red crystal bullets went straight into her back. Her brown eyes started to fade, losing much colour as life started to pass away.

"I can hear the song," she said, smiling at Philip, "I can hear his song." Her face became pale and blank, but her voice became so sweet: *"Dulu thfhulu leithflu falore halele thflo shlulu."* Her last words before her body fell to the ground.

"No!" Philip cried out as the ramp door locked shut. He rolled himself to Nanni, both in floods of tears. He held her so tight burying his head around her.

"I'm sorry," she muttered snivelling, "I didn't want to leave my Hara alone. I named her Rija. I didn't want to lose her." Philip kissed her and stayed in an embrace with her as long as he could.

Sago made his way to the cockpit. In a matter of minutes, the ship was taking off and on route to Aurelia.

# Chapter VIII

〜⌒〜

WITHIN DAYS, THE SHIP had left the Dorian system and entered the Gang of Saltus, it was announced by Sago. Philip rushed to the cockpit where Sago was on the helm. Philip looked out in awe at the sight, it was exactly as Mandel had described it: coloured gasses like dust of bright orange, yellow and red floated around everywhere, the blackness was being hidden by it. Rays of white light were bursting through illuminating all that was around them. It really was quite the sight to behold. But he felt this might be his last time in space and through the Gang. Something other than space travel seemed to be calling him.

The journey had taken nearly two weeks. In that time, Philip had gotten to know the other children who had escaped with them: Suki and Nichole were the youngest two, only four and five full suns' orbits. Then there was Leanora, Janae, Carver, and Gideon who were all around the same age as Nanni and Kaison in between Nanni and Philip's age.

The bulky lad with ginger hair was called Mayson. He along with Reenie and Trevleyan were the oldest of those who had escaped. Each one shared their story as to what they had suffered and then how they came to meet George and Tabatha. As each story was told, Philip kept hearing Tabatha's last words repeatedly in his thoughts: *"Dulu thfhulu leithflu falore halele thflo shlulu."* He wondered what it meant. It was the same language he himself had heard in the bar with Rija and when finding the old temple; it puzzled him.

Nanni and the younger children had started to play with what toys they had all rescued. There was generosity flowing, with each child sharing willingly their toys for each other to play with. Cody had started to act as a guardian to them all and loved every minute of it. For the first time in a long time, she was smiling.

The journey gave her an opportunity to really get to know them all. She was hoping when they got back to Aurelia, she would be able to stay in touch with them and be a part of their integration into Aurelian society, if there was one. No one really knew what would happen next, not even Sago knew, he was just the delivery driver.

Cody left the other children to play for a while and sat down with Philip on the grated metal floor. It was uncomfortable to sit on, but there wasn't much else. All that was in the ship was goods Sago was going to be trading elsewhere. A room had been designated for them all to sleep: there were no windows to look out into space, only walls of black or dark grey, Philip couldn't tell. Each person had a mattress, if they were lucky, it only had a few holes in it, but it was better than what they had had in recent times and welcomed the comfort and the chance to be given food knowing it wasn't going to be taken away from them. While some of the other older ones stayed in the room chatting away about what they would do when they got to Aurelia, that was Philip's cue to leave. He hadn't wanted to discuss it with them, mindlessly speculating on what they wanted when really they would do what they are told. That's when Cody sat down beside him. "You ok?" She asked softly.

Philip didn't answer at first, his open gaze tilted sideways with his neck slanted taking the weight. Taking a deep breath, he then sighed. "Yeah," answered Philip casually. "Just thinking about George and Tabatha. And what they gave up just to get us off the planet. They didn't need to help us, they could have got on the ship themselves and headed home. But they chose to help us all, we who have nothing to give them or reward them with.

"Even in Tabatha's eyes as she died, there was no hate, no regret, but a love and a joy even at the point when she had given her life just to save my sister. How can I repay them?" Philip asked.

"Only you can answer that honestly," Cody responded, "I only knew them for a short while, less time than you. But what I learned is that they wanted to give you all another chance, the chance you all deserve to live your life, something that you weren't going to get on Lepans."

"Why us? Why not some others?"

"By the sounds of things and from what I have gathered these last few days is that there probably were others. And I imagine they would have kept going."

"Until they went after Nanni. I should have…"

"Don't blame yourself," interrupted Cody. "Nanni and you are not to blame for what happened there. The guards didn't have to shoot, they could have quite easily fired a warning shot, but instead, they shot to kill. They are the ones that killed them."

"They wouldn't have been there if…"

"You can't say things like that because it will eat you up inside and devour all the goodness in you. It's more than likely they would have stayed and who's to say they might have been caught then and been given a worse fate. They knew what they were doing, they knew the dangers they faced and faced them with love and compassion."

"What about all those they could have helped and saved? Who will help them?" Philip asked, still hurting.

"Well, I believe the love and goodness they have shown, would not have gone unnoticed, and it is quite likely someone else will pick up that mantle and bear it until their time comes when another picks it up, and so it will go on until Lepans is freed, or there are no more people to rescue," replied Cody. Out of her pocket she took out a small handheld leather bound book, a little smaller than Philip's hand. "Tabatha gave this to me." Philip looked at it. The leather had been well worn and some of the fragile pages stained from the oils of the fingers. "The Amel Cristea," remarked Philip.

"She asked me if I could find her son John and deliver it to him and tell him they love him very much. But I'm sure they wouldn't mind me giving this to you. You look like you need it more than I do," Cody jested.

"Will you tell their son what happened?"

"I will try, but I have no idea how to find him.
But I will try."

"She said he is in the fleet. You could start by
contacting them," suggested Philip.

Cody smiled and left him to his thoughts. Philip
flicked through the pages, not really reading anything,
but just looking at the words to see what Tabatha
had read. He saw passages and words underlined,
reading those one specifically.

The ship entered the Ionian system. Aurelia was
only a few days away. Along the journey, Philip had
done little to admire the ship he was in. Once there
were days when he would long to be up in space flying
in a ship across Jubal, going from system to system
and planet to planet, seeing all kinds of nature that
he had not seen before and the vastness of space in
all its wonder. But now as he reflected on his earlier
dreams. Now, he didn't know. The life of his saviours
had affected him greatly.

The next few days went by. He spent much of it
reading the book he had been given.

Carefully going through passage after passage,
skipping through it again, but reading intently the
passages George and Tabatha had marked.

He came to a familiar book: *The Songs of Anani*.
Just as Philip remembered his father's Amel Cristea,

both marked and underlined the same passages all over, but one in particular stood out amongst the many:

*You are the melody, where the universe is in harmony. You are the giver of light. The song of worlds who sings for me, let me keep singing in your harmony. The darkest night can't hide your light.*

Shouts came from other parts of the ship. Shouts of excitement and joy. "It's Aurelia! Aurelia! Come and see!" The young children's voices shouted.

Philip followed and was the last one to the helm. There on the viewer screen ahead above all the holographic controls was a spectacular sight of a green, brown and golden sand planet, with oceans vast and wide as sapphire blue as they come. Above the planet two of three space stations could be seen, Aurelia's Gates. Dotted all around the planet were cloudy grey, white lighthouses relaying a protective shield across the entire planet, powered by three space stations orbiting the planet.

It was such an amazing sight to see, at times they all wondered if they would ever see this day. There was much excitement filling them, even Nanni had started to get excited, still holding Rija the Hara tightly under her arm. "It's so beautiful," Reenie commented, her honey eyes staring in wonder and her light brown straight hair falling, still in the moment.

Philip felt the sunlight of the Ionian sun hit his hand with the Amel Cristea in. He turned it over to the front leather-bound cover. There for a moment he saw scratched into the leather scribbles, or was it something else, he couldn't be sure, but the light from the sun lit the markings up further:

Philip was struck with something he couldn't explain, it was like he suddenly understood.

*"Dulu thfhulu leithflu falore halele thflo shlulu."* He muttered to himself. The sun shone brightly, he squinted as he caught the rays shining on Aurelia and the ship as it approached the station of Burloca. "Be the light for all to see," he mumbled to himself.

The ship approached a metropolis-sized station. Sixteen long rectangular structures, eight on the top half, eight on the bottom half, all fitted together in an octagonal shape, with corridors wide enough for four people to walk side by side heading into the middle of the station where a square structure sat under a dome of whitened grey. On each of the eight sides were long tunnels big enough for a city size Sun of War to fit into.

Sago instructed the children and Cody to gather what little possessions they had and prepare to disembark, while he landed the ship down on the vast platform amongst other private and commercial ships.

The ramp fell. With disbelieving eyes, they wandered, admiring and almost slack jawed at what was in front of them, but more so, that they had made it to Aurelia.

"What do we do?" Mayson asked the question all were thinking. Sago had started to unload his goods and almost became unconcerned for them; he had done his bit. There was probably little else he could help with.

"Let's go and find someone," Cody suggested taking the lead, holding the hands of the two youngest children. Philip held Nanni's hand, who was still holding Rija the Hara by its neck under her arm.

All the children's eyes gazed around at the vast space station bay. It was the size of some of the harvest fields on Lepans where a number of them had helped out over a full suns orbits past where they had lived.

They headed through the long corridor to a large foyer and travellers' gateway. Cody went up to the desk, where a man dressed in a black suit with a smaller jacket contrary to the ones they had seen the Ranians wear and what they knew was in fashion on Aurelia. "Can I help you?" He asked politely.

"We are refugees, we have just escaped from Lepans. We need help and we need to tell the authorities here what is happening over there. Hundreds are being killed and executed for no reason; it's genocide almost," Cody pleaded.

"Refugees? So, you have no travel documents and you are not registered here on Aurelia?" The man asked.

"These children no longer have a family. So no, they don't have travel documents," Cody replied, getting herself worked up.

"Ok, bear with me for a moment. I just need to get my supervisor." The man headed off. Soon he returned with a woman dressed in a similar executive suit. She had long blonde wavy hair and high heels that clicked on the stone-like flooring.

"If you could all come with me," she said in a soft voice. She smiled, but it didn't look like a sincere one, more like a forced polite smile that she has to give.

They were all escorted to her office. The view looked out over the planet with part of the long arms of the station on view. After sitting down at a desk, she activated the holographic computer. Words and numbers in mid-air appeared selected and moved by her fingers.

"Right, what I'm going to need to do…is to take down all your details. Once I have all of that. It will be sent to the Carseld office in Vortigern. Once everything has been processed, the children will all be sent to different homes and orphanages, anywhere that's available."

"Can we not all be together?" Cody asked.

"I'm afraid it doesn't work like that. First come first served. It has to go to the next available place and that could be anywhere on the planet. We do obviously make exceptions for siblings, but otherwise there is nothing else I can do. As for you, Madam, you will be given a temporary apartment, again wherever is available. You will of course be assigned an officer to help you with your readjustment into Aurelia. There is a bit of a backlog, so things might take a little time to process. While we wait, temporary accommodation has been made available in a shelter in the city of Burloca. It's the best we can do I'm afraid."

"How long will this take? We need to see the Senate, or someone in authority. They need to know what is going on on Lepans. People, Aurelians are dying, being slaughtered," Cody demanded.

"I'm so sorry," the blonde executive said. While she might have looked sorry, behind it she wasn't, it was just words, words to please a politeness that ignored the real issues. "I'm afraid that's not our responsibility, if you wish to contact the Senate, then you will need to find out who your nearest Senator is once you have been relocated."

"How long will this take?" Cody demanded. "Again, I'm sorry, but there is a backlog. It could be a few weeks, possibly a couple of months. I honestly can't give you an exact answer. We will of course transfer you as soon as possible to the planet surface once a transport ship is made available. That should be by the end of the day. If not the first thing tomorrow morning. Now I will need to take down as much information as you can give me."

Dumbfounded and lost for words, Cody answered the lady's questions. Then the other children answered. The smaller ones gave little as they knew very little, only as far as their parents were 'mummy and daddy.' All names, family members and ages were recorded, along with any medical information they knew of, which for the majority of them was nothing.

It was Philip's turn. He sat down with Nanni on his lap holding her Hara, gently rubbing the ear with her finger and thumb again to soothe her.

"Could I have your name please?" The lady said still with her well-spoken voice. She had done fifteen of these before, each one taking a long time, her impatience was growing along with the children's. Still, she put on a front to mask her annoyance.

"Creda...Philip and Nanni Creda," Philip replied.

"Thank you," the lady said. "Do you have any family...?"